The Secret Of Moon Lake

The Secret

OF

Moon Lake

SOFIA NOVA

Illustrated by Marina Terkulova Tesch

Registered and catalogued with the Library of Congress - ISBN: **978-0-578-59944-1**

First Edition. Printed in the United States of America

ACKNOWLEDGEMENTS

Thank you, God.

For giving me the power and strength to pursue my dreams. I could never have done this without the faith I have in you.

To my father, Dr. Gerry Gunter Tesch,

For revealing to me the knowledge of the Kingdom of Light and Darkness.

You've inspired me with everything you have done and especially your belief in me.

To my mother, Marina Tesch,

For showing and teaching me the beauty of art, wisdom and the power of love.

To both of my brothers, Jonathan and Benjamin,

for keeping me adventurous and full of laughter...

But especially for my little munchkin, "Benji".

Contents of The Secret of Moon Lake

The light of the full moon shone brightly over the shimmering water. Its reflection peered through the leaves, revealing a silhouette of a dove cooing sweetly. To anyone it was a beautiful yet eerie setting, but little did anyone know there was a secret... a secret yet to be told.

After a while, the ripples from the water calmed. A glowing white figure slowly sank. Deeper and deeper into the water, until there was no more. The wind came to a still. The dark clouds slowly covered the bright full moon, leaving Moon Lake to a silent black night.

CHAPTER ONE

Swept Away

There is something very eerie about watching rain hit the water from underneath. With his lungs begging for oxygen, Sam Lawrence knew this had to be the end. He kicked and paddled frantically.

The underwater reeds felt like hands pulling at his feet, holding him captive in the depths of the lake. With all his might, he tried to untangle himself from the dense reeds. He felt a tight pain squeezing his chest, as a wave of dizziness swept over him.

However, in the midst of his chaos, he thought about earlier that day, when everything was so simple and perfect. The day before his life changed completely...

***

The sunlight crept through Sam's bedroom window, waking him up. The songs of birds filled his room, then the smell of bacon.

"Come and eat!" his father called from downstairs.

Mmmm smells delicious! Sam thought.

He put on his jeans and t-shirt, and then sat on his bed to put on his socks. He looked up into the full-length mirror on the wall, opposite his bed. Sam's eyes were the color of honey. The handful of freckles on his cheeks were darker now that spring was around the corner and the weather was getting hotter. He patted down the hair sticking up on the top of his head, but soon gave it up as a lost cause. No matter what he did, his hair just stood up at odd angles.

"The lake will be perfect today," Sam thought out loud, as a huge smile burst across his face.

He had made sure that his best friend, Ethan, would join him at Moon Lake to go fishing. Yesterday, they had been at the lake all day. Ethan's parents never let him out on school nights, so now was their only other opportunity to fish for the legendary "Big Bass."

Sam's mouth tightened in concentration. Maybe today was the day he would catch Big Bass! People had been trying for years. Sam thought as he looked at himself in the mirror.

If I finally caught Big Bass, everyone would know about it. I'd get my picture in the local paper. And even Jessica, at school, would finally notice me and then…

"The food's getting cold," his dad called from downstairs.

Mr. Lawrence tried to make a family breakfast every weekend. Today he made his son's favorite breakfast: bacon and waffles. Sam chased the smell of bacon across his room, dodging his skateboard and video game controllers scattered on the floor. He raced down the stairs and even leaped the last four steps. He wouldn't let anything delay him getting to the lake.

As soon as he sat down at the kitchen table, Sam dove right in. First, he devoured the bacon and then swallowed the waffles in a couple of bites.

"Sam!" his father exclaimed. Little bits of waffle batter splattered onto the floor as he shook the big, wooden mixing spoon at Sam. "You didn't wait for the rest of the family, and you didn't pray for your food."

Sam frowned. "But Dad, that takes too long," he whined, "Plus. I have to get to the lake ASAP. Ethan's waiting for me."

"No, there's always time for prayer. Be more patient," his dad insisted.

Sam rebelliously mumbled a few words before finishing what remained on his plate.

Mr. Lawrence looked at his son with the eyes of an understanding father. Even when he was upset with Sam, he still had a kind face. Sam's father was the sheriff of Moon Lake, but today was his day off. He stepped over, tousled Sam's hair, then turned back to the waffle griddle.

It really isn't fair, Sam thought. *I want to be fishing already.*

"Dad, can I use your fishing rod?"

Mr. Lawrence shook his head as he pulled a waffle off the griddle with a fork.

"That's for the big fish. I only use that to go deep-sea fishing. Maybe you can use it when you're more grown up."

Sam exhaled in disgust at the words, *grown up.* If he could only catch the famous bass, then he could prove to everyone who lived by Moon Lake that he was a real man. If today was the day, he had to get moving.

Quietly sneaking out of the kitchen, he entered the garage, pulled his bicycle out and raced down the driveway with his bait box and fishing rod. Down the street, Ethan's face brightened when he saw his best friend riding towards him.

Ethan was already waiting on his bicycle at the end of his driveway. Ethan's bike was a hand-me-down from his big sister. It was pink with white polka dots. To make matters worse, it even had a wicker basket in front and purple streamers on the handlebars. Ethan's sister had given it to her little brother under one slightly mean condition—that he didn't change it at all.

Ethan was the same age as Sam, fourteen, and they had been in the same classes in school since kindergarten. Ethan wasn't very popular at school. Partially because he always spoke his mind, and that tended to get him into trouble with the older kids.

It was also partially because Ethan was a bit overweight and constantly looked like he had just woken up. His clothes were always rumpled. Of course, Sam didn't care about any of those things. He loved Ethan like a brother. Best of all, Ethan loved fishing almost as much as he did. Just like Sam, Ethan also carried his fishing rod as he rode his bike.

Ethan started pedaling as Sam approached his house. There was no need to stop and chit-chat — they both wanted to get to the lake as quickly as possible.

"Today's the day!" Ethan shouted as Sam caught up to him, riding down the street.

"Big Bass is ours!" he replied with glee.

The boys rode down a few streets, Ethan now huffing and puffing to keep up. Then they parked their bikes at the beginning of the trail to Moon Lake, right next to creepy old Mr. Brown's house. The big rocks and roots on the dirt trail were tough on bikes. Wild vegetation and tree branches blocking the path made it much easier to walk.

Carrying their fishing gear, the boys started walking. Within just a few minutes, it was like they were in the middle of nowhere. The boys took off their sneakers and tied the laces together, hanging them over their shoulders. There were no sounds of cars or people, just the forest. Birds sang to each other as they flew from pine to fir trees.

To Sam, the forest looked like huge Christmas trees all crowded together. The trees were so dense that they formed a canopy high in the air. The forest underneath was shaded and cool.

Still, some rays of sunshine filtered through the pine needles and made watery shapes on the ground, as the smaller trees swayed in the wind. Not a single cloud was in sight. For Sam, it was perfect. It was Saturday, there was no homework to do tonight, he was with his best friend—and they were off to catch Big Bass.

Sam took a deep breath. As he held his breath, he let the forest aroma fill him up inside. Finally, he exhaled with a sigh. In his excitement, he started walking faster. The tall green grass felt like fine silk slipping between his bare toes. Ethan quickened his pace to keep up.

"Yo. What bait are you using today?" Ethan asked.

"I'm probably just going to net some shiners from the lake."

Shiners were baitfish and super easy to catch. Sam could usually catch several of them with one throw of his net.

"Mind if I borrow a couple lures?" Ethan asked.

Sam nodded in response as he looked down at his bait box, swinging in his hand. Sam's bait box was his treasure. The case itself was a dull metal color with a wire handle. It was a little battered, but that was only because it was so old and well used. Originally, it had been his grandfather's. Grandpa had passed it down to Sam's dad, and Sam's dad had passed it down to Sam.

He had every detail of the inside memorized. It opened up like a toolbox, with three rows of compartments. On the bottom were the different sized metal weights and sinkers.

Then came the row of tools—pliers, cutters, fishing hooks—and extra fishing lines. Then, in the top row, were the real treasures: the lures. The lures were attached to the end of the fishing line, the parts that fish bite onto. Some of them were so old that Sam's grandfather had made them.

After just a few more minutes of walking the trail, Ethan and Sam arrived at their fishing spot on the docks of Moon Lake.

No one really knew how Moon Lake got its name. Most people in the state of Maine thought the Native Americans, who used to live there, named it. The name made sense, though. The lake was almost a perfect circle, connected on one side to a stream, and on the other to a larger river that eventually led all the way to the ocean. Moon Lake was so big that you could hardly see the other side.

The creepy side, as Ethan had called it before. The far side of the lake was overgrown with trees and bushes, so people kept away from it. Some of the elderly residents even said it was haunted.

Sam and Ethan walked onto the single dock, jutting out into the water. Some people swam here, but you had to be very careful. There was a notoriously strong current that pulled swimmers towards the connecting stream and eventually the ocean.

There were also many clumps of water grass and reeds that made swimming even more difficult.

In many spots at the end of the dock, old fishing line was tangled around rusty nails. A few wooden planks at the end of the pier were decaying, so you had to know where to step. Fishermen had fished there for as long as anyone could remember because the fish would take refuge in the reeds from the heavy current.

Sam and Ethan picked their way carefully between the rotting boards. Sam put his bait box down near the end of the dock and quickly set up his fishing pole. Ethan did the same.

"Watch me catch Big Bass!" Sam laughed as he threw his fishing line far out into the lake.

"I'll catch him before you do," Ethan challenged.

For hours, Sam and Ethan laughed at each other's jokes and stories. They threw their nets into the water and pulled out shiners. At one point, Ethan caught a small bass, but not big enough, so he let it go back into the lake. In fact, the boys had so much fun that the hours passed quickly and they did not notice the large, dark clouds creeping in from the east.

A few drops of rain drizzled onto the dock. Sam sniffed the air. He could smell something metallic and electric. A tiny chill raced down the back of his neck. He looked at Ethan. Ethan realized the same thing Sam did, at the exact same time.

Ethan whistled. "Look at those clouds."

"A storm is coming," Sam replied. "A big one."

The trees swayed back and forth against the howling wind. Moments later, rain began pouring down in buckets. Sam watched huge drops of rain bounce and splash off the dock's wooden boards. Instantly, the boys were soaked. It was raining so hard, so fast, that streams of water were running down Sam's bangs and into his eyes.

"Ethan!" Sam called out over the pounding rain. "Grab your stuff. Let's get out of here!"

Even though Ethan was only a few feet away, Sam had to shout to be heard over the rain bouncing loudly off the dock and lake.

The dark clouds overhead were already covering the entire lake in shadow, as if it were night. Ethan raced to pull his fishing line in from the water.

Sam grabbed his rod off the end of the dock, but when he did, he felt his line catch on something underwater. He jerked on it a few times, but it wouldn't budge. Then, with one mighty heave, it suddenly came free, surprising Sam, and he lost his balance.

"Ethan!" Sam screamed. "Help!"

At the same moment, a brilliant strike of lighting hit the trees on the creepy side of the lake. The loud bang of the thunder followed immediately, shocking Sam into truly losing his balance for good. Flailing his arms, Sam stumbled backwards off the dock. Before he knew it, he was underwater–along with his bait box and fishing rod.

The strong current pulled Sam into the depths. Dense reeds began to tangle between his legs as he kicked and paddled frantically. It felt like something had wrapped its hands around him, pulling at his feet.

The water was so brown and murky that Sam couldn't see more than a foot or two in front of him.

Although his visibility was blurry, all he could see beneath him was a mess of brown and black reeds wrapped around his legs. He pulled at them with all his might.

Then he caught a strange glimpse of something long and silvery flashing beneath him.

It was so surprising that Sam shouted underwater — and lost his last remaining bit of oxygen.

CHAPTER TWO

The Medallion

Sam felt a tight pain in his chest as a wave of dizziness swept over him. Another flash of lightning struck and the sound of thunder rumbled a few seconds afterward. Underwater, Sam looked up and saw the surface above being pelted with the pouring rain.

The heavy rain drops looked like a million tiny fireworks exploding above.

His chest was burning for oxygen.

When he grabbed the reeds, they sliced into his hands like sharp knives, but he finally felt his legs break free. Sam kicked with his feet as the current kept tugging, trying to keep him under.

Finally, Sam's head broke through the surface of the lake and he gasped in a huge breath of air. The rain was falling so hard that he also gulped a mouthful of rainwater. He started treading water as he looked around for Ethan.

The current was so strong that he was mostly heading sideways. It had already taken him far from the dock.

"Ethan! Ethan!" Sam shouted. "Help me! I'm over here!"

But Ethan was too far away and Sam drifted even farther. The pouring rain sounded like an army of tiny cannons as it hit the surface of the lake, drowning out the sound of Sam's voice. He could see Ethan turning frantically, looking around. Ethan's mouth seemed to be opening and closing, but Sam couldn't hear Ethan's voice at all.

Then he watched Ethan start running for the trail.

"Oh no! He didn't see me fall and thinks I already left!" Sam said out loud to himself.

"Ethaaaaan... I'm in the water!" Sam called out again.

Wait. Maybe he will see my bike at the end of the trail and then come back here?

Sam felt a moment of hope, but quickly lost it again when he saw the dock grow smaller and smaller. He struggled to stay afloat, coughing and catching his breath. He kicked his legs with all his might and paddled with his arms, trying to get back to the dock.

This can't be the end, Sam thought. *Can it?*

Then the voice inside his head gave him the idea to flow with the current.

Don't fight it, the voice told him, *just float.*

So he stopped struggling and floated silently on the surface of the lake. The drops of rain stung his cheeks. Sam took a deep breath, closed his eyes and tried to stay calm.

He let himself go as he floated in the water, not resisting the strong current. He didn't know how long he floated for, but it seemed like hours. Just as Sam was exactly on the opposite side of the lake from the dock, the current disappeared. Finally, he felt the sand under his feet.

"Thank God!" he cried out loud as he quickly swam through the reeds, toward the shore. Now the rain weakened and fell lightly. It kissed his cheeks as he stood, waist high in the water.

Sam looked around slowly. A thick, gray fog was covering the lake. He could see trees by the water, clutched together like a wall, roots tangled together like gnarled fingers. Sam definitely hadn't been to this part of the lake before. Peering through the fog, he could tell that these trees were older and taller. For some reason, everything looked darker and more primitive on this side. Through the fog, he slowly scanned this new area for any danger.

Where am I? Sam wondered. The smell of wet mud filled his nose.

Raindrops dripped down from the leaves. Thunder rumbled in the distance. Sam reached for a large branch above him and pulled himself onto the shore. Birds fluttered out of the trees when he stepped on a branch and broke it.

The rain had stopped completely, but now it was starting to get dark. The crickets began chirping and the frogs joined in as well. It was like they started a musical concert. Then he noticed something in the distance. A shape that wasn't a tree. He squinted his eyes.

Sam walked into the forest to get a closer look and immediately felt an eerie presence, like someone was watching him.

He stopped and looked around, but there was nothing. Sam's heart beat faster and his breathing grew heavier and deeper.

Pressing past his fears, Sam slowly approached the shape until he was close enough to see that—it seemed to be a small cabin.

As he reached the cabin, he realized it was actually a broken-down boathouse. The dull, grimy window was almost impossible to see through, but something must have shattered the top of the glass. On his tiptoes, he was able to peer through the dark hole. Inside, he saw a long shape stretched across the floor.

"*A canoe,*" Sam realized. "*I wonder who it belongs to?*"

When Sam walked to the front of the boathouse, he found the door already open, hanging on its hinges. Mold and vines were growing all over it. Once inside, he realized that the boathouse must have been very old.

Rotten barnacles hugged the bottom of the canoe, and spider webs completely covered its interior. The floorboards squeaked as he walked from one side to the other.

Then the floor beneath him collapsed. Sam screamed at the top of his lungs. Dust spurted into the air and mud swallowed his feet.

"Ugh!" Sam shouted in disgust. He was up to his ankles in the thick mud. His head was just poking above the boathouse floor. He grabbed the floorboards above him and luckily, they weren't too rotten. It wasn't easy, but Sam pulled himself out of the hole.

Panting and kneeling on the floor of the boathouse, Sam brushed himself off, but his feet were still caked with black mud.

"This place is disgusting," he said to himself as he inhaled the musty smell of mold. Sam turned to look down into the hole he had just climbed out of and something caught his eye — something shiny, half buried in the mud.

Sam reached down and stretched out his arm as far as he could. Finally, his fingers wrapped around the object and he pulled. The mud made a sucking sound as it slowly released the shiny object, almost like it didn't want to let it go.

To his surprise, what he found was a medallion on a thick bronze chain. Mud covered most of it, but he wiped a little bit off with his fingers. In the center was a huge jewel that looked like the galaxy. It was a deep turquoise, mixed with purple, blue and green. Around the jewel, the medallion looked like it was made out of bronze. Its sides were engraved with strange markings.

"Wow!" Sam gasped, in awe.

As he looked into it, Sam felt like he was slowly spinning and falling into a colorful spiral, hypnotized.

Sam rubbed it with his fingers as he looked at it even closer.

The medallion was incredibly beautiful.

Sam felt unusual with the medallion in his palm. He was excited and numb at the same time, almost like there was some sort of magic going on with the medallion. But that was silly. Sam shook off that feeling.

"Looks like treasure," Sam said, smiling, "This should be in my collection."

It was at that moment that the forest went dead still.

Sam quickly put the mysterious medallion into his pocket.
The frogs stopped croaking.
The crickets and birds stopped their chirping.

The entire forest was muted.

Sam shivered as chills ran down his spine. He could feel his heart beating heavily beneath his chest, as his arms and legs tensed.

The silence made him feel extremely uncomfortable.

Even though he didn't see anyone earlier, he felt that eerie presence again, like someone was watching him.

The hairs on the back of his neck were standing straight up and suddenly it felt like someone had brushed a feather against his ear. Sam instinctively swatted at the side of his head.

He tried looking out of the boathouse and into the dim light to see if anybody was actually watching him from the forest.

Big Tree. Small Tree. Another Tree. Nothing...
...Okay... I think I'm good.

Suddenly, a loud, piercing noise came from the woods, like someone was dragging long nails across a chalkboard. It was high-pitched and horrifying, sounding as if an animal was screeching in pain, or maybe even shouting a warning. The supernatural sound echoed from one side of the forest to the other and then stopped abruptly, leaving Sam in silence.

Another floorboard cracked and he stumbled a few feet, almost falling back into the muddy hole in the floor. He regained his balance just in time.

"I'm out of here," Sam said out loud. His heart beat faster, thumping against his chest, "This place is freaking me out!"

Sam bolted from the abandoned boathouse and through the dark forest as fast as he could. His adrenaline kicked in as he made his way through the bushes, dodging spider webs and tree branches.

As Sam ran, he turned to take a quick glimpse over his shoulder, just to make sure nothing was following him out of the woods. Of course, with just his luck, his shoe caught onto something, causing him to fall directly into the wet mud. Sam felt his elbow jolt as his skin was painfully pierced by something sharp.

Sam yelped and saw that a gash had opened on the bottom of his elbow from a jagged tree trunk.

He carefully rose and brushed off the mud that remained glued to his clothes. As he began to dust himself off, a large arm came from behind Sam and grabbed his shoulder.

Sam opened his mouth to scream for help, but before a sound came out, the man suddenly gripped him tighter, with one arm around his waist, tight like a rope, and the other hand cuffed around his mouth.

Sam tried to scream, but nothing came out besides tiny squeaks. A nauseous sweat broke out as the palm of the man's hand held Sam's jaw tight. He felt helpless as the man pulled him up from the ground.

"Don't scream. Stop, don't scream, boy," the man said as Sam yelled into the palm of his hand. Sam 's vision cleared and he slowly stopped screaming. The man pulled his hand away. Sam spit the salty taste off his mouth, then shook the dirt off his pants and elbows.

"Are you okay?" the man asked with a deep voice. Sam turned around and found himself staring into a pair of eyes. It was the Moon Lake's police chief.

Sam gasped, "Chief Larson?"

Sam's dad was sheriff of the county, but Larson was chief of the town. Sam never really liked him with his thick, gray beard and unusually squinted, dark eyes. Or maybe it was that Chief Larson never really liked Sam. Unlike Sam's dad, Chief Larson never smiled. Ever.

"What are you doing way out here, boy?" Chief Larson said as he scanned the area with a suspicious look. Sam swallowed hard. His clothes were still damp and cold.

"I fell in the water while I was f-f-fishing on the docks and the current took me out h-h-here," Sam said nervously.

For a moment, Chief Larson considered the story as he scratched the stubble on his face. Sam could sense that the Chief didn't entirely believe him.

Sam's vision veered off toward the center of the lake. It was nearly invisible. The lake's surface was overpowered with a dense, eerie fog that hovered above. He couldn't tell how far the other side was.

Then two people, a man and a woman, gathered behind Chief Larson. The woman, Sam knew. She was Officer Darby. But Sam didn't recognize the man who was holding what looked like some kind of metal box in his hand.

Sam watched the man focus on the box. "Wave frequencies are higher in the northern direction, Chief. That is probably what caused a disturbance in the reading."

The man seemed a little odd. He spoke with a slight accent. He had a long, sharp nose and wore round glasses.

"Look who we found out here," Chief Larson announced.

"Who? What did you find?" The man's eyes darted around with high alert, as if on the lookout for danger. Then the man let out a sigh as if he seemed disappointed when he realized that they only found a boy in the woods. He carefully examined Sam up and down.

Sam stood in silence, feeling like a deer in headlights. He wasn't quite sure how to respond to the Chief's remarks or to this strange man looking at him.

Officer Darby broke the awkwardness. "It's Sheriff Lawrence's son. Are you wounded?" She asked grabbing his arm and inspected his cut. "Poor boy, you look cold. Here, take this." Officer Darby untied a warm jacket from around her hips and threw it around Sam.

"Did you see anything—unusual?" the man holding the metal box asked.

"Uh, no," Sam quickly replied, as he turned his gaze to the ground. He wanted to ask them about the strange sound, but he was afraid to mention anything that would *open the gates to endless questions*, as his father called it.

"Hmmph," Chief Larson responded.

"Well. You should be more careful," the strange man added with a smirk. "It's dangerous out here. Especially when it gets dark."

Sam froze. He had a hollow feeling in the pit of his stomach. That blood-curling sound that had come out of the forest was still ringing through his eardrums.

Chief Larson stroked his beard with his fingers, lost in thought, then he turned to aim another dark glance at Sam.

"Regardless, you shouldn't be in this part of Moon Lake," Chief Larson said as he peered out into the forest as if he was looking for something. "There have been too many weird instances with this forsaken forest."

Officer Darby shook her head as she disinfected Sam's wound. "Don't scare the boy, Chief. We should be thankful that we found him before it got too dark."

She wrapped a clean cloth around his elbow.

"He could've been attacked by a wild animal or even pulled underwater with that deadly current."

Sam nodded silently. He put his hands in his pockets and felt the medallion. Oddly, it was warm to the touch. As Sam grasped it, he felt a little surge of energy through his body. It felt powerful, almost like it were alive.

Sam knew that he didn't want to tell Chief Larson, or any of them about his new treasure.

What were they even doing on this side of the lake? Did they know about that strange high-pitched sound that had suddenly come from the forest?

Sam thought to himself, *I don't want anyone to know about my medallion. I don't know why but – I'm going to keep it a secret...*

CHAPTER THREE

The New Kid

It was twilight when Sam came home. Chief Larson personally drove him. Before Sam even got to the front door of his house, his mother embraced him tightly and became overwhelmed with tears.

"I'm so happy that you are safe! We just got the call from Officer Darby. We were so worried about you."

His mother embraced him with a tight hug. It almost felt like she hugged him until his eyes would pop out. Sam coughed and before he could say a word, his mother was already on him about catching a cold.

"Get inside and change your clothes! You need to warm up before you get sick."

His clothes still drenched and dripping wet from falling into the lake. With each step he took, his shoes squeaked with water in them.

At that moment, his sister, Leah, walked into the dining room. Leah was much older than Sam. She was seventeen. Today, she wore a light, burgundy dress and Leah's long, dark hair flowed perfectly over her shoulders.

She had a headband holding back her bangs, accentuating her bright, green eyes. Sam hated to admit it, and his friends always let him know that his sister was pretty.

"Well, looks like you almost caught Big Bass. Did it pull you in the water?" Leah teased.

From the kitchen, Mrs. Lawrence interrupted, "Make sure you don't forget to put all your wet clothes in the dryer. And give your friend Ethan a call back. He came here looking for you."

At that moment, Sam saw a reflection of sunlight dance on the kitchen walls. Curiously, Sam looked out the window and saw a large white truck parking in the driveway across the street.

"Oh, new neighbors," Leah said sarcastically as she sat down at the computer desk, "*sooo* exciting."

Sam continued to watch as a black SUV pulled up behind the truck and parked across the street. The backdoor of the car opened.

A young, brown haired boy with glasses got out and looked around, blinking at the setting sun. The boy was wearing a blue sweater with a diamond pattern on it, brown slacks and loafers. Leah stopped browsing the internet and then looked outside the dining room window.

"Look at those clothes," Leah let out a giggle, "That little kid looks like a businessman," she said.

Then a man and woman, must have been the boy's parents, exited the car as well.

The woman had a pleasant, smiling face. She put her arm around her son and whispered to him as they gazed at their new house. There was something odd about the man, though... Sam thought he recognized him. The man moved like he was in a hurry. He rushed over to the movers who had just opened the back of the truck and spoke to them quickly. It was at that moment that Sam realized that this must be the same man who was at the lake rescue. The strange one, who held the metal box in his hand.

Leah turned to Sam and raised her eyes at the man across the street. "Not like we don't have enough weird neighbors on our street. Just great," Leah sighed, turning back to her computer, unamused.

Sam noticed that the movers were now carrying one piece of furniture after the other into the house across the street.

Antique chairs and couches, beautiful mirrors with textured frames, golden lamps and aged wooden tables. Everything looked so old, like it all belonged in a museum. Then came masses of large canvases with oil and watercolor paintings. Most of them looked fierce, dark and ancient. Strange mythological creatures were painted on them like dragons, unicorns, griffins.

Sam looked out the window for the longest time. To him, it seemed like it was the most exciting thing happening in Moon Lake since winter break. Then another boy, taller, stepped out of the car. He looked to be about Leah's age. He wore black jeans, a black t-shirt, and his dark hair smoothed down neatly. He wore big headphones and walked over to his mother with a smooth rhythm to his steps.

"Looks like there's a new friend for you too, sis. Hee-hee," Sam teased. Leah looked outside again and Sam noticed how the older boy had already caught Leah's eye. Leah watched, tilting her head and twisting her hair in between her fingers.

"But his hair's worse than mine," Sam laughed.

"It's gel, you little goofball," Leah sighed. "Your hair's messy. His is stylish."

Mrs. Lawrence looked down at Sam with a loving smile. "Sweetie, don't waste your time watching others. Go outside and have your own adventures."

Sam smiled mischievously at the idea of his own adventures.

"But first change into dry clothes," his mother added.

***

The sun had already set, leaving the remaining clouds to reflect darker shades of orange, reds and purple tones. The crickets began buzzing through the trees and bushes.

Sam and Leah leaned against their own garden fence as they watched the movers unload the truck. The boy across the street made a few trips himself, carrying things. Each time he reached the truck, he paused and looked over at Sam and his sister, curiously.

Leah teased her little brother. "So are you going to just stare at them?"

"No, I just wanted to find the right opportunity to say hello."

Leah rolled her eyes and finally, Sam walked across the street. Leah followed a few steps behind as her brother approached the boy.

"Do you need any help? We're your neighbors, next door."

The brown haired boy seemed confused and didn't look Sam in the eye. "Oh, hello. Thank you, but I'm not quite sure that my parents will allow it." He had a light but strange accent, and pushed his glasses up on the bridge of his nose while he spoke.

But just at this moment, the boy's mother came outside and asked in a much stronger accent, "Did you already make some new friends, Alex?"

"Umm... I don't know," Alex replied, unsure and skeptical, "but these kids want to help us."

Leah twisted up her mouth and said, under her breath so only Sam could hear, "*Kids?*"

"That's lovely," Alex's mother said gently, "I'm Mrs. Fisher."

The woman wore a long, flowing skirt that covered her feet. It had a swirling, colorful pattern and when it moved around her legs, it almost looked alive. She wore a white shirt with tassels and many long necklaces that reached down to her waist. Her dark brown hair was long and wild. Without asking his sister, Sam knew exactly what Leah would call Mrs. Fisher—a hippie.

"I'm Leah and this is my brother, Sam," Leah said, offering her hand, "we live right across the street."

Alex's brother came out of the house on his way to the car.

"Marcus?" Mrs. Fisher called as she shook Leah's and Sam's hand. "Come and meet our neighbors."

Marcus strode over, pulled his headphones down from his ears, and grinned at Leah. He looked like he was eighteen.

"Marcus," he said in a strong accent. Leah shook his hand gently.

"You like music?" Marcus asked.

"I like your accent," Leah said.

"Let me show you the music I make. I am a popular DJ in Romania," Marcus said. He smiled and waved Leah over to the car. Marcus placed his headphones on Leah's ears and hit play on his cell phone. Leah's eyes lit up. She started nodding her head in time with the music in her ears.

Mrs. Fisher smiled and turned back to the younger boys. "I'm sure that will keep them busy for a while. Here, why don't you grab these pieces." She handed Alex and Sam each a small box, then went over to speak with the movers.

Sam followed Alex up the driveway and through the door. Sam was intrigued as he looked around the house. There were brown boxes all over the wooden floor, stacked up on one another, and plastic coverings on the walls. Although it was a huge mess, the large pieces of antique furniture, the couches and tables, stood in their places.

"I'm sorry it's so untidy," Alex said embarrassedly. He studied the floor in silence, "but, I'm sure you understand, we're just moving in."

"Sure I understand," Sam said. He scrunched up his face, unsure why Alex sounded so sophisticated when he spoke.

Finally, Alex glanced shyly at Sam. "You said your name is Sam?"

Sam smiled, "Yeah. And you're Alex, right?"

"Yes, that's right, Alex Fisher."

"That's the coolest name," said Sam.

"Why?" Alex replied, confused.

"Because that's a good reason to be a fisherman!"

"I never went fishing before," Alex scowled at the thought.

"Oh, then you've come to the right place. I'm an expert fisherman. We can even go fishing this week!" Sam was bouncing on his heels with excitement.

Alex went back to studying the floor. "Thank you for the invitation but I have to prepare for school. So not this time."

Sam frowned in disappointment. "Too bad," he said under his breath.

"Follow me please," Alex said. "These belong up in my room."

The boys made their way up a gigantic grand staircase at the left side of the large entry room. Even the upstairs hallway was already crammed full of boxes. Just outside Alex's room, Sam noticed the other room across the hallway. It looked like it had already been set up.

Sam noticed a crack of light seeping through the half open door. He paused and tried to take a sneak peek at what was inside. There were several big desks covered in strange technical equipment of all sorts and a massive computer screen covering nearly an entire wall. The other walls were covered in sketches of dark, creepy-looking mythical creatures, just like the ones in the big paintings Sam had seen being carried into the house, earlier.

"Ahem..." Alex cleared his throat. "Sam?"

"Oh, sorry," He immediately turned around.

"This way please," Alex said, directing him to his own room.

The room was empty, apart from Alex's bed. The boys set their boxes down.

"So you moved from another country?"

Alex sat down on his bed and said, "Yes. Well, we lived before in a country called Romania. My family is half Romanian and half Scandinavian."

"Wow, Romania and Scandinavia? I never heard about those places," Sam added, his eyes gleamed.

"We lived in is a fairly large city in Romania called, Bucharest," Alex said, "my mother thought that the life in a smaller city, like Moon Lake, would be much better though."

"Is that why you moved?"

"Well, not completely," Alex said with a shrug. "The main reason is because my father has a new job in this area. So we're here."

They heard Mrs. Fisher's voice as she walked up the stairs. "Now, where are my little helpers? Both of you disappeared." She entered Alex's room and asked, "Do you want to eat something?"

"No thanks," Sam shook his head, "my mom is already cooking dinner."

Alex stood up from his bed, "Well then. It was indeed wonderful meeting you and your sister. Maybe I will run into you at school on Monday, Sam."

Sam tried to be formal as well, and shook Alex's hand, "Yes, sir."

Alex was caught off guard and didn't know what to say, so he pushed his glasses up and raised his eyebrows.

"I'll catch ya later," Sam said with a laugh and walked out the doorway.

He paused in the hallway to peek into the strange room again. Something about the mysterious room drew him to it. Just as he leaned in to get a closer look through the half-closed door, Sam saw Alex's father inside the room spin toward the door and rush over. Mr. Fisher's dark, beady eyes glared at Sam just before he slammed the door in Sam's face.

"Oh!" Sam said. It was at that moment, he realized he was right. Alex's father was the man who accompanied Chief Larson and Officer Darby at the lake earlier.

Suddenly, Alex's mom was behind Sam, staring at him. Her lips were pulled together tightly into a frown. "The stairs are that way," she said, pointing.

"Right! Sorry!" Sam ran down the stairs and out the front door, like something was chasing him.

The sky turned dark, all the streetlamps were lit, leaving an orange tint on the streets. He saw his sister standing in front of their house. He rushed to her and came to a stop, panting.

"What's wrong with you?" she asked, raising one eyebrow.

"Nothing," he said, catching his breath, "Just getting some exercise. How's Marcus?"

"Cute. A little odd but cute. And he's got great taste in music," Leah said, chewing her lip. "But the rest of them are kind of weird, right? Especially the father?"

Sam thought of Mr. Fisher slamming the door in his face. A shiver ran down his spine.

"Nah," Sam said against his own judgement, crossing his arms. "As a matter of fact, I think Alex is kind of cool."

Leah raised one eyebrow in disbelief. "Cool?"

"He's different," Sam said, defensively. "Interesting… and at least he's not totally boring, like Julia."

Leah's eyes narrowed at Sam's comment about her best friend. Then she rolled her eyes and shook her head. The siblings walked inside their house and headed upstairs to their rooms.

Sam hadn't wanted to admit it to her, but Leah was right. There was something odd about Alex's family, especially his father. What were all those hi-tech gadgets in the other room? Why had Mr. Fisher slammed the door when he was trying to peek in? But Sam already knew he liked Alex. Maybe he would be a new friend after all.

Just as Leah closed the door to her room, Sam had made it to the top of the stairs and stopped.

That's when he overheard the words from his father saying, "…and they told me that they received another report, this afternoon, just before Sam was found. We haven't heard of this kind of occurrence in Moon Lake for nearly fifty years."

"What do you mean?" Mrs. Lawrence asked concerned.

Upstairs, Sam didn't understand the first few words, so he leaned over the rail to hear what his father was saying.

"…We don't know where or what it's coming from…" Mr. Lawrence paused and picked up his sheriff's bag, "I don't understand. It's like some kind of an echo, and we simply can't pinpoint the source."

Mrs. Lawrence comforted her husband with a hug and a soft voice, "Don't worry, love. Don't put this extra stress on yourself or the department. I'm sure it's just a strange echo. Maybe some kind of animal. Nothing the neighborhood should concern themselves with."

Sam bent down, because he didn't want them to know that he overheard his mom and dad speaking to each other.

Mr. Lawrence then straightened himself and he said in a much stronger voice, "No... it can't be. The reports are becoming more frequent and the residents are afraid. They want answers! We are supposed to protect them."

Sounds coming from the lake?

Sam whispered under his breath, "What exactly are they talking about?"

The stair beneath Sam's foot creaked, and his parents both looked up at the stairway. Sam's heart stopped. He could feel his cheeks turn red. Thinking fast, Sam acted as causal as could be and began walking down the stairs.

"The house smells great, mom! What are you cooking?"

CHAPTER FOUR

Beautiful Reflections

"A-Achoo!"

As the other children milled around the classroom, socializing, Sam sat at his desk and wiped his nose on his sleeve. Sam knew he was coming down with a cold. It was no big surprise after getting lost in the freezing lake.

Last night, Sam's dad made him promise never to go back to Moon Lake after sundown. The current was obviously very dangerous. Begrudgingly, Sam had promised. He and Ethan usually finished up their fishing before the sun went down anyway.

Today, the clouds and drizzling rain outside made the whole school feel kind of empty. The icy, moist air certainly wasn't going to help Sam's cold.

The school bell rang loudly, signaling the start of class. Mrs. Hulbert was apparently running late, so the students spoke amongst themselves, but most of them surrounded Jessica Avalon, one of the most popular girls in the seventh grade.

Sam stared at her out of the corner of his eye, trying not to be obvious about it — but he couldn't help it.

Jessica was a tall brunette and wore a different dress to school almost every day. In Sam's eyes, she was the most beautiful girl in the world.

"I heard that the new kid is from another country," Jessica announced with a smile. Her two girlfriends, Briana and Stacy, giggled. From his seat next to Sam, Ethan piped up.

"Do you even know where this new kid is from?" Ethan asked, laughing.

The entire group looked briefly at Ethan and then stared right back at Jessica. Sam nudged Ethan with his leg and shook his head. Jessica wasn't used to being challenged. However, there had been a feud between Ethan and her for three years now. Ever since she led the class into laughter when the school bully, Tommy, pulled Ethan's shorts down in gym class. Whenever he could, Ethan tried to embarrass her—which annoyed Sam to no end since he had a crush on Jessica since the first grade.

Jessica gave Ethan a snooty look in return and said, "You know what Ethan? If I were you, I wouldn't say something that clueless. I heard he's from Bolivia." The entire group around Jessica was in awe.

"Wow, Bolivia?" one girl squealed in excitement.

"No way!" another boy said.

"You know what?" Ethan mimicked in a high-pitched voice. "You probably don't even know where Bolivia is."

"Mmmph… I actually know *exactly* what I'm talking about," Jessica said, flipping her hair over her shoulder and turning away from Ethan.

"Yeah." Jessica's girlfriends agreed with her and then all three started whispering and giggling, throwing occasional dirty looks at Ethan.

The teacher, Mrs. Hulbert, suddenly entered the room and cleared her throat loudly. The class was immediately quiet. Mrs. Hulbert sat at her desk.

"Good morning, children," she said in an assuring voice, "today we want to begin our day with reading. Please pick up your textbook and turn to page eighty-seven."

The sound of shuffling pages was heard throughout the room as each student turned to the article. Sam opened up his backpack to reach for his textbook. He noticed something glowing at the bottom of it.

It was the medallion! It looked so magical, shining brightly with its blue-green aura. Sam nearly had to cover his eyes. This time it shined even brighter than yesterday.

Wow. What kind of medallion is this? Sam thought. *I don't even remember putting it in my backpack!*

"Sam," Mrs. Hulbert suddenly said. The whole class turned to glare at him. The blue-green glow from the medallion at the bottom of his backpack reflected up on Sam, giving his face a strange, blue tint.

Sam looked up at the teacher.

Now his face was a mixture of blue—and red, from embarrassment. Sam felt his ears grow hot.

"Please turn off your cellphone." Mrs. Hulbert had assumed that the strange blue light on Sam's face was coming from a cell phone in his backpack. "This is the only warning you will receive."

At first, Sam felt a flush of anger. With his hand buried in his backpack, clutching the medallion, he didn't feel like he had to listen to Mrs. Hulbert at all.

The medallion was his.

He should be able to hold it if he wanted. It was more important than any stupid reading they would do in class today…

"Sam?" Mrs. Hulbert repeated, more sternly. From across the aisle, Ethan kicked Sam in the foot, shocking him. Inside the backpack, Sam dropped the medallion.

He realized he was breathing heavily. Now, he didn't feel quite as frustrated with Mrs. Hulbert as he had a moment ago when he was holding the medallion.

"Oh, I'm sorry," he said nervously. He pulled out his textbook and quickly closed his backpack.

"Please start reading from where we stopped last time," Mrs. Hulbert said as she put on her reading glasses and turned to her textbook.

He took a deep breath and was about to begin his sentence when suddenly a loud knock was heard at the door.

The principal stepped into the classroom, followed by Alex. Principal Marvin was a tall, slender man. He had a sharp face with an awkward, high-pitched voice. Principal Marvin greeted Mrs. Hulbert with a warm smile and a wink — all the kids knew that the two had been dating for about a year — and then apologized for interrupting. Principal Marvin then turned his smile to the class.

"Good morning," Principle Marvin said. The class greeted him in return.

"Today I would like to introduce you to a new student at our school. His name is Alex Fisher. I hope all of you will be friendly to him and give him a nice welcome."

The class was quiet. All thirty pairs of eyes were observing Alex, curiously, from head to toe. Alex fiddled with his fingers and stood there silently. Briana whispered to Jessica, "He looks like old man Marvin's little clone!" The two girls giggled quietly.

Sam didn't like anyone whispering mean things about his new friend, but he had to admit — it was true. Just like Principal Marvin, Alex was wearing dark slacks, a white button-down shirt, and a blue suit jacket with little corduroy patches on the elbows. As if on cue, both Principal Marvin and Alex pushed their glasses up onto the bridges of their noses at the exact same time. The girls giggled again.

Mrs. Hulbert walked over and placed her hand on Alex's shoulder.

"Let's see where we can find you a nice place to sit."

She scanned the classroom as she looked for an empty seat. Principle Marvin glanced at the clock on the wall, and then he gave Mrs. Hulbert a flirtatious smile.

"I have a meeting to attend, Mrs. Hulbert. Have a lovely day…"

Mrs. Hulbert blushed. As Principal Marvin left the classroom, she quickly straightened herself up.

"Oh here! An open desk, right next to Ethan." Mrs. Hulbert pointed her finger at the desk towards the back of the class. A little unsure, Alex maneuvered himself to his seat and then suddenly noticed Sam who was sitting on the other side of Ethan.

"Oh, it's you, Sam. I had no idea we would be in the same class."

Sam greeted Alex with a high five as Alex sat down at his new desk.

"You two know each other already?" Mrs. Hulbert asked with a pleased smile.

Sam turned to Mrs. Hulbert and replied, "Yes. As a matter of fact, we're neighbors."

Alex nodded in agreement.

"Okay then. Well, I hope you will find yourself welcome in my class, and I don't believe it will be that difficult to make friends here. Right class?"

"Yes, Mrs. Hulbert," the class droned together.

"Pardon me, Alex, but you seem to have an accent I cannot place," Mrs. Hulbert continued. "I'm rather curious to know where you are from. Is it a large city?"

Alex cleared his throat. "Yes, Mrs. Hulbert. My family and I moved from the city of Bucharest in Romania."

"Wait, from where?" Ethan asked innocently, turning his eyes to Jessica.

"Bucharest," Alex said again.

"Oh Bolivia, you say?" Ethan said in a much louder voice.

"No, Ethan. I said I'm from Bucharest," Alex stated, louder and with a hint of frustration, not sure why Ethan made the mistake.

Ethan rubbed the bottom of his chin with his thumb and pointer finger. "Hmmm… for some odd reason, I thought someone said you were from Bolivia. I just can't remember who it was… oh wait, I think her name was Jessica." Ethan grinned as he sneered a mischievous look. The entire class turned to look at her too. Jessica blushed.

"Uh no," Briana snapped back in defense of her friend, "I'm pretty sure she said Bucharest. Maybe you should have your ears cleaned, Ethan."

"And your hair," Jessica whispered just loud enough for a few kids to hear, but not Mrs. Hulbert. A handful of students starting cracking up.

"Okay everyone, settle down," Mrs. Hulbert said. "Let's move on with our article. Sam? Will you begin reading please?"

He sighed and gave Ethan one last shake of his head. *Why does he have to antagonize Jessica all the time?* he thought... but Ethan only grinned back.

***

After school, as soon as they sat down on the bus, Sam finally got to say to Ethan what he had been waiting to mention all day.

"Bro, why did you say all that to Jessica? You know I like her."

"Say what?" Ethan asked, shrugging his shoulders. He pulled a chocolate bar out of his backpack.

"You know what," Sam said in a serious tone. Ethan took a huge bite out of the candy bar then, giving Sam a slightly disgusting view of half-chewed chocolate, said, "What? Bolivia? Bucharest? Whatever."

Sam shook his head in frustration. Ethan's eyes grew big and round.

"Come on, I was just messin'. You know I'm never serious about that kind of stuff. She just can't take my humor." Ethan's teeth were now smudged brown from the chocolate.

Sam thought to himself for a moment, then said, "I know… but sometimes if you don't have anything nice to say, maybe you shouldn't say anything."

"Sorry, I just couldn't help it. Bolivia? Really?" Ethan laughed and accidentally dropped the chocolate bar on the ground.

"Awe, man," Ethan said, saddened as he picked up the chocolate. He carefully examined the tiny hairs and dirt now stuck to the candy bar. Ethan turned to look out the window and his face brightened when he spotted Briana outside the bus. She wasn't paying attention to anything but her phone.

"Eat this!" Ethan exclaimed as he threw the dirty candy bar right at Briana. The candy bar landed on her head and instantly stuck to her hair! Briana screamed.

Ethan sat right back down in his seat, licking his fingers, acting as if nothing had happened. Sam had been too lost in thought even to see what had happened with Briana. Still, Sam knew that Ethan had a crush on Briana, though he found strange and interesting ways to display it.

"Jessica's so gorgeous," Sam mumbled. "With her luscious hair and beautiful hazel eyes. Once you really get to know her, she's actually nice."

"Nice?" Ethan couldn't believe his ears. "Ha! She's fake! I can see right through her 'beautiful brown eyes'."

"Come on, man, that's not fair," he pleaded. "Maybe that's just how you see it."

Ethan squinted his eyes at his best friend. "You only like her 'cause she's the prettiest girl in school. Admit it."

Sam could only blink at Ethan, not knowing what to say.

"Don't judge a book by its cover, man," Ethan said, shaking his head. Sam opened his mouth to speak but at that moment, Alex walked up onto the bus nervously and looked around for a seat. Sam got up and waved.

"Over here Alex! We saved you a seat."

A small smile of relief crossed Alex's face. He walked down the aisle to Sam and Ethan, pulled his backpack off, placed it under the seat, then sat down and straightened his back.

"Thank you for your consideration," Alex said, nodding formally. The bus left the school parking lot and began its route. At every new community, a few students were dropped off at the stop. Sam stared out the window, lost in thought. The trees were glowing as the sunlight dried the water droplets off their branches and leaves.

"Listen, Alex," Ethan said as he leaned over closer.

"I'm listening, dear friend," Alex said.

Ethan rolled his eyes. "Dear friend? Alex, this is exactly what I mean. I know you're foreign and have the accent... but common. You aren't that sophisticated."

Alex raised one eyebrow. "Sophisticated?"

Ethan breathed in slowly and then exhaled. "Would you please just stop with the formality? I'm about to puke!"

Alex pulled his head back in shock. "Excuse me? I'm a highly educated individual and I have no desire to-"

"See!" Ethan interrupted him abruptly. "Can't you just relax a little bit? Stop being so uptight! We aren't meeting the president. We are your *friends*." Ethan then punched Alex on his arm.

"Ow," Alex hissed, then raised his hand. "Okay, fine, Mr. Bolivia. Whatever you say."

"Hey, it wasn't even me who said that," Ethan snapped back. "I was making a statement about Jessica."

Sam, caught in the middle of the two, felt the urge to bring balance into the situation.

"Alex, don't get offended. We're your friends. Ethan just means that he feels like you aren't comfortable with us."

Ethan leaned back into his seat and Alex crossed his arms over his chest. Neither one was budging an inch. Sam continued. "Alex, we're playing soccer over at the twins' house before dinner. Come join us."

"Hmmm, I suppose," Alex said. "I do love soccer and it has been a very long time since I've enjoyed the game."

Behind Alex's back, Ethan was mocking his serious tone by moving his lips along to Alex's words and acting like some high and mighty king of the universe, waving his arms around with his nose in the air.

Sam kicked Ethan under the seat and Ethan cracked up, silently. The bus came to its second to last stop. The two boys got off the bus along with a few other students.

Ethan waved from the bus as it pulled away. "I'll see you guys soon!" Then, looking at Alex, Ethan continued, with his nose pointed to the sky and an improvised accent, "I shall be looking forward with great anticipation and eagerness until we three shall meet again!"

This time, even Alex cracked up laughing.

"See you soon!" Alex and Sam both responded.

CHAPTER FIVE

Strange Movements

Sam walked up to his driveway. He saw Julia's new white car parked out front. Julia was Leah's best friend and they were inseparable. Sam inspected the new car from all angles before entering the house. It was shiny and spotless.

He smiled to himself as he remembered the conversation his dad had with Leah before school that morning. When Julia had picked her up for school, his dad came outside to ask Julia how long she had her driver's license. Mr. Lawrence's face turned white as a sheet when she smiled and said, "One week!"

The same day Julia had passed her driving test, her wealthy parents had bought her the car. Leah rolled her eyes when her father extracted a promise from Julia to drive extra safely, as driving a car was no joke and took practice and care.

As soon as Sam entered his house, he sighed in relief, knowing that he only had about a half-hour of homework to get through before he could go play soccer.

The aroma of fresh-baked chocolate chip cookies filled the entire house and made his mouth water.

As he followed his nose toward the kitchen, he saw Leah, Julia, and Alex's brother, Marcus, sitting on the couch watching TV with a plateful of cookies on the table.

"Hey Munchkin!" Leah exclaimed. "We made chocolate chip cookies."

"I can smell them," Sam said as he sniffed the air. His stuffed nose seemed to have gotten a little better since the morning.

"You can have some, if you like," Julia said, not even looking up from her phone.

"Marcus came over to show us his new music track," Leah said with a slight laugh. "It's amazing," she added, patting Marcus on the knee. Marcus blushed.

"So happy you like it," Marcus said kindly in his thick accent.

Sam noticed how Leah was growing more and more friendly with Marcus. *That's okay with me*, Sam thought. *Marcus sure seems a lot nicer than the brainless jocks Leah and Julia usually hang out with.*

"Guys, be quiet!" Julia shouted. "This is exactly what I was telling you about today, Leah. Look!" The television was showing a blonde female reporter from the local news. She was standing on the shore of the lake. Sam could see his fishing dock behind her.

"There have been many reports throughout the entire community of Moon Lake," the reporter was saying.

"Some older residents remember the same strange sounds happening fifty years ago, back when someone gave them the very mysterious name, 'The Yearning.'" The reporter grinned, making light of the creepy sounding name.

"Here's what one resident had to say…"

The screen showed a full-figured woman with large sunglasses. She spit onto the ground and then said, "You know, I was minding my business. Smokin' a cigarette in the backyard, and uh, you know all of a sudden I heard, uh… this creepy sound. Like a dying animal or somethin'. Then it gets louder and louder and after a minute or two, poof — it's gone. I've lived in Moon Lake for thirty years now and I ain't never heard of no ghosts haunting this lake. But ever since the beginning of this month, these noises happen every single night. It's a sign!"

The screen changed back to the female reporter wearing a small smile. The reporter cleared her throat.

"A sign? Maybe it's a sign that the wind is picking up these days and making some strange sounds coming through the trees."

The reporter paused to smile at her own words before getting serious again. "At the moment, local authorities are looking deeper into the cause of this eerie epidemic. Now back to you, Chuck, for this weekend's weather!"

On screen came the local channel's weatherman, Chuck, in his shiny green silk suit and a thin moustache. "Eerie epidemic indeed!" he chuckled. "Now let's see what sort of strange and mysterious weather we'll enjoy this weekend!" Chuck winked at the camera.

Julia grabbed the remote off the table and muted the TV. "See?"

But Leah and Marcus weren't listening. They were sharing a set of headphones, listening to Marcus' song, and smiling at each other.

Julia rolled her eyes and went back to obsessing over the texts on her phone.

Sam grabbed two cookies off the plate, then ran upstairs to rush through his homework. As soon as Sam walked into his room, he opened his backpack and reached in for a book. Instead, his hand came out with the medallion.

He looked at it closely. It shimmered with blue and green. The medallion was so beautiful. Sam thought he could stare at it forever and never get bored. Just like last night at the boathouse, as he held the medallion, Sam started feeling warm. Strong. Confident. He felt like he could take on anything at all. Underneath that sense of strength, though, was a strange dizziness. He felt like he was falling straight into the medallion, like the swirling blues and greens of the beautiful jewel were pulling him in...

Then he heard it. Like a whisper coming from far away.

"Sam... Sam..."

What the... am I hearing things?! But yes, it sounded like someone was whispering his name. He turned to look all around his room. No one, nothing. He heard it again, and again it sounded like the whisper was coming from far away ... and ... underwater? A little freaked out, Sam quickly placed the medallion on his desk.

"Sam? Are you okay?"

He jumped at the voice and realized his mother was in the doorway of the room. She smiled.

"Sorry, honey, I didn't mean to shock you."

His mother walked up to him cautiously. Sam turned around, grabbed the medallion off his desk, and put it in his pocket.

"What's that?" his mom asked, nodding at Sam's pocket.

"Nothing."

Mrs. Lawrence raised her eyebrows but also smiled. "Nothing, huh? All right. So how was school? Did you do okay on your test?"

"Uh… test?" Sam asked nervously.

"Yes, didn't you have a test today?" Mrs. Lawrence sat down on Sam's bed. She pulled his soccer ball from the corner and held it in her hands.

In his pocket, out of sight, Sam clutched the medallion. "Yeah, I did great," Sam said confidently.

"Oh good. I'm so proud of you." Mrs. Lawrence smiled, comfortingly.

Sam's eyes grew narrow. He took his hand out of his pocket and ran his fingers through his messy hair.

Why did I just lie to her?

"Actually, Mom, I mean... no," Sam said. "The test is tomorrow."

Mrs. Lawrence cocked her head to the side. "Honey, are you okay? Your nose sounds stuffed. I hope you didn't catch a fever."

His mother raised her hand to check his forehead. Sam stuffed his hands back into his pockets. Again, he grasped the medallion. It felt warm. Strong. He felt himself grow angry. *Why does she treat me like such a child?*

He flinched, pulling his head away, and then he snatched the soccer ball out of her hands.

"No!" Sam said loudly. "Stop it! I'm fine!"

Sam's mother's eyes went wide in shock. She had never heard her son raise his voice at her in such an aggressive manner. Ever. Mrs. Lawrence stood up immediately.

"Sam Lawrence. Don't you speak to me like that! That is disrespectful."

Sam looked at his mother and realized what he had done. He shook his head.

"I-I'm so sorry, Mom," Sam stuttered. "I didn't mean to raise my voice. I don't know what came over me."

At that moment, Mrs. Lawrence's phone rang. She let out a sigh.

"I have to take this call, honey. But really, that kind of behavior just isn't called for. We can talk about this later."

Then Sam's mother's face softened as she left the room with her phone.

Sam shook his head and pulled the medallion out of his pocket. He gazed into the gemstone. Already, he loved it very much. It was the most beautiful thing he'd ever seen. Well, maybe next to Jessica.

Sam sighed. He would do his homework after dinner. For now, he was upset with himself for lying and just wanted to get out of the house.

He put the medallion into his desk drawer.

Just as he was about to close it, he saw the jewel in the medallion sparkle.

It hit his eye brightly, like a reflection of the sun.

Sam slowly reached out to it, to take it into his hands again, but stopped abruptly— hearing his sister's laugh from downstairs shocked him out of it.

"Hmm... this is getting weird..." he slammed the drawer shut, grabbed his soccer ball, and ran out of his room.

CHAPTER SIX

The Map

Sam walked outside. A cold breeze swayed the large green trees on the street. Birds chirped and screeched loudly like a broken orchestra.

He opened his backpack and took out his new soccer ball. The wind blew again, chilling Sam to the bone. He let out his breath in a shiver. Sam even thought about going back inside and calling his friends to say the game was off.

As he was looking into his backpack, Sam froze. There it was again, at the bottom, a tint of blue-green light. The medallion. Just as before, he didn't remember putting it in his bag. He reached in and took the medallion into his hand. Warm energy spread out from his hand, down his arm, and into his chest. Suddenly, he didn't feel cold at all. In fact, he felt great! He was full of energy and ready to take on *all* his friends in a soccer game, all by himself.

Sam grinned as he stuffed the ball into his backpack, and ran across the street to the Fisher residence. As soon as he reached the big double doors, he pressed the doorbell twice and waited, tapping his foot. He couldn't wait to get playing.

Mrs. Fisher opened the door. She had no makeup on and was dressed in a long purple dress with an apron tied around her waist. She had a colorful handkerchief with frilly tassels wrapped around her hair.

"Hi Mrs. Fisher, is Alex in? We were going to play soccer."

She smiled. "Hello, Sam. Yes, Alex is home. He loves that game." Then, more seriously, she added, "Let me see if he finished his homework."

Alex had heard the doorbell and called out from the top of the stairs, "Almost done, Mother! Sam, you can come up here if you want." Alex turned and disappeared down the hall.

Mrs. Fisher moved aside and Sam entered the house. He tossed his backpack over his shoulder as he climbed the stairs, sneaking a glance at Mr. Fisher's office, but the door was closed.

Once he entered Alex's room, Sam noticed that it was already set up and unpacked. Nice and cozy.

Without looking up from the homework, Alex said, "Hey there. Just one moment."

Sam sat down on a small chair. "What are you doing?"

"Oh, there's only one more math problem to solve," answered Alex. Sam waited quietly as Alex concentrated on his last question, pushing his glasses closer to his eyes. After a few seconds, Alex suddenly slammed his textbook closed. Shocked, Sam jumped a little in his chair.

"Whoa, is everything okay?" Sam asked. Alex spun around on his swivel chair and grinned at Sam.

"Yes! I can't wait to play some soccer."

Alex hopped over to his closet. "I haven't played in such a long time!" As Alex began replacing his shiny leather shoes with old, beat up Converse sneakers, Sam looked over at Alex's desk. "You sure finished that math problem fast. I wish I could do…"

Something had caught Sam's eye. It was a big square of paper, tattered on the corners and yellowed with age. In fact, it looked ancient, like something an archeologist would find.

"What's this?" Sam asked.

Just as he was reaching for it, Alex darted over and snatched it up. "Oh, uh…" Alex said with unease, "that's just uh… my dad's map."

"A map? But for where?"

Alex seemed uneasy. He held the map behind his back. "It's just a project my dad's working on." Alex shrugged, like it was nothing, but Sam could see right through him.

"Come on… you can tell me," Sam begged, "Remember? I'm your friend. I promise not to tell anyone."

Alex thought for a moment and then sat next to Sam. He whispered, "Okay, so don't tell anyone. This is *really* classified information."

Sam nodded seriously.

"Promise?" Alex asked again. Sam nodded, quickly this time.

"So this piece of paper has a secret," Alex explained as he unrolled the map.

"A secret?" Sam studied the ancient paper. There was handwriting on it in strange, curvy lettering. It also had a big, blue circle in the middle, surrounded by trees.

"Wait a minute," Sam said. "That looks familiar. Is that…"

Alex nodded, now more proud. "Yes. It is a map of Moon Lake."

"Cool. But so what? What's the big secret?" Sam couldn't understand why it was so hush-hush.

"Viking ghosts!" Alex said a little too loudly and then quickly cuffed his hand over his mouth and looked over at his door. He brought down his voice. "What I mean is that these ghosts come out at night and haunt Moon Lake."

Sam stared at Alex for a long moment.

"Hilarious," Sam said sarcastically. "Come on, man. Viking ghosts? Nothing ever happens here in Moon Lake. I've never heard of Viking ghosts prowling around. Somebody is just trying to scare you with silly stories."

"Fine. Don't believe me," Alex folded his hands over his chest. "Soon you will know the truth and then you'll come running back to me for answers."

Sam stopped laughing and realized Alex was being completely serious.

Although he knew that his town was quiet as a mouse, Sam remembered the recent news reports about the noises at the lake.

Sam straightened himself. "Okay, so how do you know about these Viking ghosts?"

Alex lifted his head with pride and said, "My dad's a scientist. He came here to study Moon Lake. He told me there was some kind of disturbance in its water flow. And its chemical composition. Something abnormal."

At that moment, Alex's father opened the door. Sam nearly jumped. Mr. Fisher was wearing huge goggles with big magnifying glasses in front of the eyes. He looked like something out of a scary movie. He was fiddling with a few wires in his hand.

"Alex, I need your help with the computer. It's not connecting correctly…"

Mr. Fisher finally looked up and noticed Sam. "Oh!" he exclaimed. Behind the creepy glasses, Mr. Fisher's eyes looked huge!

"Dad," Alex said slowly, "This is our neighbor, Sam."

Mr. Fisher examined Sam with his magnified eyes and stared awkwardly. He didn't reveal that they had already met at the lake.

Mr. Fisher wore a long white coat with shorts. His socks were mismatched, one brown and one white, and they sat above his ankles. Between that and the glasses, he looked like a mad scientist who had just left his secret laboratory filled with test tubes, electricity machines and strange animals in jars.

"Hi," Sam squeaked nervously and then cleared his throat.

Mr. Fisher noticed the map in Sam's lap and his eyes grew even bigger. Alex grabbed the map and quickly rolled it up, trying to cover it.

"Come on, Dad, let me look at the computer. It's probably a software issue."

Staring at the map in Alex's hands, his father said with a stern voice, "Yes, I need to talk to you right now."

Alex turned to Sam and gulped. "I'll meet you outside in a couple minutes."

CHAPTER SEVEN

The Splintered Window

As they rode to the twins' house, neither Sam nor Alex said a word. Sam felt bad. Alex was sullen and didn't look him in the eye. It looked like his father had really chewed him out about something. Sam didn't want to intervene. If Alex wanted to talk about it, he would. But Sam couldn't help thinking about that ancient map. *Moon Lake. Haunted?*

The twins lived at the edge of the forest surrounding Moon Lake, on the other side of the street from old Mr. Brown's house. As Sam and Alex approached, they saw that Ethan was already there, leaning against his bike, shaking his head at Brayden and Cameron who were on the front lawn, wrestling. The twins had been born only minutes apart and were always competing over absolutely everything. They looked just like each other, with their reddish hair and tall, lean bodies.

"One-two-three!" Brayden blurted out.

"My shoulder was up at two!" Cameron protested.

"No way!" Brayden yelled. "That was three!"

"Was not!" Cameron countered.

"Was too!" Brayden called out.

"That's not fair!" they both said at the same time.

"Hey guys!" Sam exclaimed. Cameron used the distraction to kick his brother off of him. Both twins stood up, brushed themselves off, and adopted the cool, laid back attitude they were famous for—when they weren't fighting with each other.

"What's good?" Cameron said as Sam high-fived them both.

"You're Alex, right?" Brayden said. "Nice to meet you."

Alex nodded, eyes to the ground. "Pleased to make your acquaintance."

The twins raised their eyebrows. Ethan rolled his eyes at Alex's stiff greeting.

Sam tossed the soccer ball at Brayden but Cameron grabbed it out of the air.

"Ready to play?" Cameron said with a grin.

As usual, the boys used the young trees in the twins' front yard as goal posts. There were five boys so the teams would be uneven. Brayden and Cameron argued over which team should have three players, since each of them thought they didn't need a third player on their own team. Brayden and Cameron never played on the same side—they needed to play against each other. Ethan flipped a coin and it turned out to be Brayden, Alex and Ethan against Cameron and Sam.

The wind had died down and now the sun beat heavily against the boys' skin as they played. Sweat dripped down their red foreheads. Throughout the afternoon, the soccer ball went back and forth between the two teams, with lots of pushing and shoving between Brayden and Cameron. Surprisingly, Alex was a good player, just as good as Sam. It didn't take long for the twins to like Alex, especially the way he could juggle the ball very well with his knees. Alex mentioned that he used to practice a lot back in Romania.

The teams turned out to be mostly even after all, since Ethan spent as much time lying on the grass, catching his breath, as he did playing.

After a few hours of laughter and a lot of screaming, the score was tied, three to three. Sam hated to admit it to himself, but he was exhausted. He didn't know if he could play anymore. The other boys seemed to be feeling the same way too. As Sam stood, catching his breath before the final kickoff, he thought to himself, *If I could just get some energy! I don't want to lose!*

Sam closed his eyes. His breathing slowed. He dug deep into himself, wanting very much to get a boost. Then, he heard it.

"Sam…"

"Huh?" Sam looked around. No one was talking to him. The other boys were all quietly catching their breath, too.

The voice in his head returned. *"Sam…"*

Sam blinked his eyes. The voice was mysterious, but somehow familiar. Then he realized — it sounded like the voice he had heard before, in his room, when he was staring at the amulet. It was definitely a female's voice, he realized now. A very sweet sounding voice.

Sam walked to his bike and grabbed his backpack, which was hanging off the handlebars. He opened it up and the blue-green light was there again, shining up from the amulet at the bottom of his bag.

The amulet was so beautiful. The light coming from it was pulsating in waves, brighter and brighter. *"Sam..."* the amulet seemed to say in his mind.

Without thinking, he reached in and took the amulet in his hand. Again, warm energy flowed up his arm and into his chest. It didn't stop there, though. This time, the feeling of strength and confidence spread throughout his entire body. He felt it in his legs and his feet. Suddenly, he was completely energized and ready for battle. It was like he could take on anything or anyone! He put the medallion into his pocket.

Sam's feet started pumping. He was jumping up and down, in place.

"Come on, guys!" he said. "Let's do it!"

Ethan looked up, his face nearly purple from exhaustion. "C'mon bro. Just one more minute... please."

"No way!" Sam shouted. "Let's go!"

The other boys dragged themselves to their feet. Ethan shuffled over to the two saplings that designated his team's goal. He would stay put and play goalkeeper. The twins put on a show of not looking tired, but Sam knew that they were.

"Okay," Brayden huffed, "next goal wins."

In the center of the yard, Brayden kicked off to Alex. Alex dribbled toward Cameron, did a spin move, and got past him. The only thing between Alex and the goal was Sam.

Sam felt ten feet tall. Like nothing could stop him. He charged toward Alex, slid feet first, and knocked the ball away. Alex ended up on his butt.

"Hey!" Alex shouted.

Brayden and Cameron reached the ball at the same time and started kicking it—and each other's shins. Sam flew toward them, faster than he had ever ran in his life. He hit each of them with one of his shoulders. Both twins spun around and hit the grass, face first. Sam raced away with the ball.

"Sam?!" In the goal, Ethan was staring at his best friend in shock. He had never seen Sam so aggressive. Or so impressive. He hadn't done anything against the rules, but he had definitely stepped up the power and energy of the friendly game, overpowering Alex, Cameron and Brayden.

Now Sam was pacing toward Ethan with the ball at his feet and a ferocious look on his face.

Ethan took a step back. "Take it easy, man!"

But Sam was like a locomotive hurtling toward the goal—and Ethan. Sam looked not only focused and powerful, he looked downright angry. Ten yards from the goal, Sam drew back his leg and kicked with everything he had. The ball took off, right toward Ethan's face!

Ethan shrieked and dove out of the way. The ball rocketed through the air exactly where Ethan's face had been! Not only did the ball clear the twins' whole front yard, it sailed all the way across the street, climbing higher and higher into the air, until-- CRASH!

The ball went straight through the neighbor's window! The window didn't completely shatter. Instead, because the ball had been kicked with such incredible force, it went straight through, leaving a soccer ball-sized hole. The rest of the window was splintered and cracked, like a huge spider web.

Cameron, Brayden and Alex were staring at the hole in the window, their mouths hanging open. As one, they turned to look at Sam. Sam wasn't looking. He was jumping up and down, yelling, "Goooooaaaaaallllll!"

"Sam!" Ethan called. "What's wrong with you?"

Sam's body felt electric. Supercharged. But then his best friend's voice stopped him in his tracks. He stopped jumping and shook his head.

"Wait," Sam said. "What just happened…"

"You broke a window!" Cameron yelled.

"Old Mr. Brown's house!" Brayden called out. "Oh no!"

"What are we going to do?" asked Cameron. The boys grew silent looking around to see if anyone saw.

At that moment, the wind picked up and clouds rolled in from the east.

For a moment, the boys just looked at each other, their mouths hanging open. Cameron was the first to act. He ran, quick as lightning, into his house. Brayden followed close behind. Ethan jumped on his bike and raced down the street.

"Guys," Ethan shouted. "Come on!"

Alex and Sam hopped on their bikes and pedaled after him.

In the neighbor's house, a face appeared, framed by the hole in the window. It was an ancient face, weathered by many seasons, with dark brown, penetrating eyes. Deep lines ran across the cheeks, making the older man's face look much like the splintered window itself.

The face gazed serenely after the boys on their bicycles, then disappeared back into the house.

***

The boys didn't stop until they were three streets away.

"What was that all about?" Alex demanded.

"You almost took my head off!" Ethan shouted.

"Guys," Sam said, "I'm sorry. I don't know what came over me. I was just… like… full of energy. Like an adrenaline rush or something."

"Energy?" Ethan chastised. "You looked like a madman, like you were gonna kill me!"

"I'm sorry," Sam said quietly.

Ethan frowned. "Yeah well, it was a fun game until you went all Terminator. Geez."

Sam felt awful. If the ball had hit Ethan, he could have gotten seriously hurt. Plus, he had broken a window. And they had all run away! What a terrible situation!

Alex looked at Sam and Ethan, then he asked, "What are you going to do now?"

Sam shivered. "I don't know. I don't want to get in trouble. But, maybe I don't have to do anything. I don't think anyone saw what happened."

"That's right. We won't say anything!" Ethan declared.

Alex pressed his lips together. "I don't know about that… maybe we should all go and apologize. Plus, the twins live right across the street. I think this Mr. Brown is going to know who did it."

Ethan threw up his hand, brushing off what Alex had said and turned to Sam, "Nah. Just listen to me. Am I ever wrong? You don't have to say anything to nobody. Go home and act as if nothing happened."

"But what about my new soccer ball?" Sam said in distress.

"Doller store," Ethan said confidently.

Alex looked at his watch and said, "Well, I shall return home now."

"Yeah, I'm going to do the same," Ethan agreed. "Good luck, Sam."

The two boys slowly departed and Sam was left alone on the corner of the street. Slowly, Sam climbed onto his bike and started pedaling. A single tear trickled down his cheek.

CHAPTER EIGHT

Mr. Brown

Just as Sam was opening his garage door, his father arrived home, earlier than usual. He pulled into the driveway and stepped out of his police cruiser.

Mr. Lawrence called, waving. "Any new adventures today, my son?"

Sam muttered quietly, "Hey dad."

"Oh man, what's going on?" his father asked. Usually Sam greeted him enthusiastically, especially when he came home early. Mr. Lawrence peered at his son. "Something happen at school?"

Sam tensed when he heard the question. He did not want to tell his father what had happened.

Sam shrugged, "Oh no, nothing happened. Just tired."

Mr. Lawrence cocked his head but didn't push the issue. He put his hand over Sam's shoulder and they went into the house together.

The house was still filled with the sweet aroma of cookies. The plate that earlier had been full of fresh-baked cookies was now half empty. The TV was off.

Sam and his father were greeted by Sam's mother. Mrs. Lawrence began to prepare the table with cheesecake and tea. At that moment, Leah and Julia walked down the stairs. Alex's brother, followed them.

"Who's this?" Mr. Lawrence asked Leah, blinking at Marcus.

Julia blushed and answered for Leah, "This is actually Marcus. He's the new neighbor from across the street."

Mr. Lawrence's gaze did not move from Leah as he said sternly, "What did I tell you about having boys in your room?"

Again, Julia jumped in.

"Marcus was interested in the reports about those strange sounds coming from Moon Lake. You can see the lake from Leah's window, so we were just showing it to him."

Marcus reached out his hand and said in his mysterious accent, "I'm sorry, sir, I hope that's all right." Mr. Lawrence shook Marcus' hand. Marcus continued, "What do you think about the sounds coming from the lake?"

Mr. Lawrence seemed uncomfortable. "We're looking into it. You should know. Well, you seem like a nice young man. But our rule around here is no boys upstairs."

"Of course, sir," Marcus said, bowing his head a bit. "I'm sorry, I didn't know. It won't happen again."

Leah rolled her eyes at her father. "Come on, Marcus, we'll see you later." Leah and Julia walked Marcus to the door.

"Nice meeting you both," Marcus said to Sam's parents as Leah pulled him away. Mr. Lawrence frowned while his wife smiled. She tilted her head up to whisper into her husband's ear. "Don't worry. They're good kids... plus he is kind of cute."

Mr. Lawrence's eyes went wide. He watched as his wife walked away, giggling at his reaction.

***

Sam sat down on the end of the couch in total frustration. He felt uneasy. Geezer, the orange cat, was laying over half the couch with his legs and arms spread out. Sam stared at his cat as he pet him. *"Wouldn't life be easy if I could just be a cat? Eat, sleep and enjoy life without any problems."*

Suddenly, the doorbell rang.

Geezer jumped from Sam's lap and onto the floor instantly. Sam's heart skipped a beat. He could already hear his dad's footsteps coming towards the living room.

Sam yelled, "I'll get it!"

He ran to the door and looked through the peep hole. Sure enough, it was Mr. Brown! Sam's heart skipped a beat when he saw his soccer ball in his hands.

Sam swallowed hard as he opened the door slowly.

"Uh, hi Mr. Brown. W-what brings you here?"

He walked out of his house and closed the door behind him.

Mr. Brown was an elderly Native American man. He walked with a cane, except it wasn't the usual cane that older people used. Mr. Brown's cane had large red feathers tied to the end and looked more like a staff. His wrinkles sunk deep into his skin. Sam had only spoken to Mr. Brown a few times before. Mr. Brown mostly kept to himself, in his house. The twins said he had a million books in there, and all kinds of herbs and strange Native American trinkets. His rich hazel eyes focused on Sam so intensely that Sam wanted to look away.

"Young warrior," the man said. "Would you happen to know whose beautiful ball this is?"

His voice was melodic. He spoke almost like he was singing, the words climbing up and down and sounding like bird's song.

Sam was quiet. There it was, just inches away, his new soccer ball, right in Mr. Brown's delicate hands. The ball was covered in small pieces of dirt and grass marks on the side.

Finally, Sam stood up straight and said, "I'm not sure whose it is. I'll be sure to ask around though."

Mr. Brown looked at Sam for a moment and his face grew sad. Then he nodded slowly, all the while staring deeply at Sam. The wind picked up, blowing Mr. Brown's long ponytail. Sam froze. It felt like Mr. Brown was looking directly into his soul.

"Such a shame," Mr. Brown said in his song-song voice. "I can't seem to return this lovely ball to its rightful owner. I was hoping you would know to whom it belonged."

"Who's at the door?" Hearing his father's voice so close behind him, Sam closed his eyes tightly.

"Is that good, old man Mr. Brown?" Mr. Lawrence asked with a welcoming smile. Sam slowly moved aside so that his father could open the slightly closed door.

"Good afternoon, Sheriff," said Mr. Brown. His eyes seemed to dance.

"Come in, you must be cold." Mr. Lawrence welcomed him with an open arm. "It's always good to have your positive energy around."

"That's alright, Sheriff. I wouldn't want to trouble you. I was only looking for the owner of this ball."

"That's Sam's ball," Mr. Lawrence declared. "We just bought it for him."

"Is that so?" Mr. Brown's deep eyes focused on Sam as he stood in the doorway, silent. The feathered staff blew with another cold breeze.

Mr. Lawrence stared at his son, trying to understand the awkward silence. Sam closed his eyes and breathed deeply. He knew that now everything had to come out.

Sam stuttered, "U-uh... w-well..."

Of course, at this moment, Leah had to show up. She stepped out from behind Mr. Lawrence and raised her eyebrows at her sullen little brother.

"Yeah, what's going on, Sam?" Leah asked with a mischievous grin, her hands on her hips. "Is there something you want to tell us?"

Sam ducked his head down. This was the end. That was it. No escape.

Sam's dad sighed. "You'd better come inside, Mr. Brown."

***

Quietly, Sam confessed and told them the whole story. His father and the old man listened carefully and there were no interruptions, besides the occasional remarks from Leah. When Sam finished, everyone silently looked at Mr. Brown. Geezer pounced on his lap. This surprised Sam, since Geezer never went to strangers. More than that, Mr. Brown whispered something into the cat's ears, in a different language, and Geezer was purring like a freight train.

Mr. Brown cleared his throat with three short coughs. Then he faced Sam.

"I understand you, young warrior. And all is good now that you have told the truth. But there is still an unsolved problem. Who will pay for the broken window?"

Sam had not thought of this. He gave his father a questioning look. Mr. Lawrence only raised his eyebrows.

Sam mumbled, "Umm... well, I don't have any money."

Mr. Brown tilted his head. "But you have two arms. A back. And you must have very powerful legs to kick a soccer ball with such force."

Sam's father nodded. "Yes. Perfect."

Sam shook his head. "I don't understand."

"You're going to work off the cost of the window," his father told him.

"Work?" Sam gulped. Mr. Brown was an odd man. Sometimes he looked peaceful; other times he looked mysterious. Mr. Brown placed the orange cat back on the floor, carefully whispering to her some more, then stood up. "Then it is decided. There are leaves to rake. A garden to weed. And a window to replace."

"I think that's a great idea," said Mr. Lawrence.

Sam didn't think he ever wanted to step inside the old man's house at all.

Still, a weight was lifted from his shoulders. He had told the truth. Late, for sure, but better late than never.

His heart felt like it had released a heavy pressure and now he only had to rake some leaves in return. Mr. Brown agreed that the boy could come on Saturday and work the whole day.

Before leaving, as Sam was walking him to the door, Mr. Brown turned to shake Sam's hand. He had a firm, strong grip, especially for an elderly person.

Sam looked up at him and said, "Thank you for understanding. I'm really sorry this happened."

The old man smiled and patted Sam's shoulder. His face was kind but his eyes focused directly into Sam's. "Next time you should tell the truth when you have the opportunity."

Mr. Brown let go of his hand and pointed a finger into Sam's chest. "It feels better now, doesn't it? In here?"

Sam nodded as he let out a sigh of relief. "Yes, sir. It does."

The man's eyes searched Sam's. "But there is still something you keep hidden. A secret."

Sam stiffened. *How does he know? Does he know about the medallion?* Sam's mind worked furiously to respond. Just then, from far overhead, came the screech of a hawk. Mr. Brown looked up. Sam followed his eyes. Sure enough, a hawk was circling high overhead.

"Look at that," Mr. Brown said, a grin spreading across his weathered face. "She agrees with me. You are hiding something."

He tilted his head back down to stare at Sam for a moment. "I will see you Saturday, young warrior."

And with that, the old man turned and walked away.

CHAPTER NINE

The Secret Garden

The following Saturday afternoon, Sam huffed loudly as he picked up the last huge stack of leaves and pushed it into a black trash bag. Working in Mr. Brown's yard had not been as easy as he had expected. It was like a jungle!

Sam had already picked up the large sticks cluttering the sides of the house. He had rearranged the half-buried stones on the garden path. He had mowed the grass, trimmed the wild bushes with the big scissors given to him, and he had pulled out piles of stubborn weeds. The backyard seemed to be neglected for years.

Time crawled by and the work seemed to be never-ending. Finally, the sun was beginning to set. Sam sprawled out on the grass.

"There! Finally finished!"

Sam looked over the backyard and realized he had done a great job.

Where before the backyard had been one big mass of scattered sticks, overgrown bushes, and tall grasses, now there was order. At first, Sam hadn't even been able to see the stone path. Now he saw that it wound its way through the yard in a flowing, S-shaped curve, almost like a stream meandering through a meadow.

A little bird flew out of the thick bushes at the back of the property, where the stone path ended at a wooden fence masked in dense shrubs. Sam looked closer at the fence. He saw a crack running up and down the wood, and then he saw a small, rusted doorknob. There was a gate in the fence. He hadn't noticed it before.

"I wonder what that could be?" Sam whispered. Sam got up from the grass, brushed the dirt from his knees, and walked towards the back bushes. He twisted the doorknob, expecting it to be rusted solid and stuck, but it spun freely in his hand. He pushed and the gate door opened smoothly and silently on its oiled hinges. It was strange. It looked like it hadn't been used in decades but the gate was in perfect working order.

Sam ducked under the bushes, walked through the gate, and then stood with his mouth hanging open. He was in a secluded garden. It was huge, just as big as the entire backyard.

While the other yard had been a jumble of wildly overgrown plants, this secret garden was precisely arranged and perfectly ordered. There were rows of evenly planted vegetables: tomatoes, squashes, pumpkins and all kinds of other colorful vegetables. All of them though, looked plump, healthy, and about to burst open.

There was also a herb garden with tall stalks of rosemary, basil, and many other aromatic herbs that Sam had never seen before. In between all the veggies and herbs were rose bushes in full bloom.

Sam inhaled deeply, his nose filling with the delicious smells of rich earth and delicate flowers. He shook his head.

Why would Mr. Brown let his yard get so chaotic and messy, yet keep this secret garden all to himself?

A swift breeze blew through his hair. Sam noticed rocks on the ground, making a walkway. Unlike the flat black stones in the yard, these sparkled in the afternoon sun with specks of gold and silver. Sam followed the path with his eyes and was surprised to see that it led to an old shack. Sam hadn't noticed it before because it was covered in ivy and blended in very well with the rest of the garden.

Slowly, Sam walked up to the shack. He tugged on the wooden door. It swung open freely, just like the hidden gate. The wooden door creaked loudly as it banged against the shack.

"Whoa," Sam whispered.

The walls of the shack were covered with wooden shelves, and the shelves were jammed full of old books. Old wasn't the right word for it. The books looked ancient, like they belonged in a museum. Many of them were covered in a thick layer of dust, like they had been sitting there for many years, untouched. Others had a shiny look to them which Sam took to mean they had been read over and over, and recently.

Against the back wall was an old wooden table. The only thing on it was a faded yellow notebook. Sam opened the notebook slowly and began to flip through some of its old pages. There were pencil sketches of plants and animals with cursive writing scribbled on the side in a language Sam did not recognize. Every page he turned had another sketch: a hawk, a rabbit, a fish, lily pads, and even some of the herbs he saw out in the secret garden. Time flew by as Sam studied the pages, lost in thought as he looked at all the beautiful illustrations and mysterious notes.

"So, I see that you have found my artwork, young warrior?"

Sam spun around to see the old man standing in the doorway with his feathered staff in his hands.

"Oh… uh… yes. I mean sorry. I know I shouldn't have been looking through your things. I couldn't help it."

Mr. Brown looked at him kindly. "My boy, it's alright. A wise man once said, 'The important thing is not to stop questioning. Curiosity has its own reason for existing.'" Mr. Brown placed his hand on Sam's shoulder. "Follow me curious one, I would like to tell you a story."

The two walked through the secret garden, back through the hidden gate, across the backyard, and up to the house. Mr. Brown leaned heavily on Sam as he climbed the three steps onto the back porch. Then the old man grabbed his rocking chair and slowly sat down. Sam looked around and found a nice spot to sit on, a little rug by the steps. For a long time, both were quiet and did not say a word. Breathing heavily, Mr. Brown looked up at the sky. Different kinds of birds sang to each other from one branch to the other. Now that Sam had gotten a chance to get to know Mr. Brown a little better, he wondered if the old man actually was in good health. Just the short walk from the shed had made him very tired.

Mr. Brown kept looking up at the sky. "I can hear the question in your heart, young warrior. You need some time to learn, like all of us, but your question is a shrewd one."

"What question? I didn't ask a question."

"Your heart did. And your eyes. And your feelings are correct. My days on this earth are numbered."

Sam blinked, afraid to hear any more. "What do you mean?"

Mr. Brown took a deep breath and closed his eyes before he said, "I am very old. Older than you think. No one lasts forever."

The news hit Sam hard. He felt it in his heart, a heavy weight. He had not spent much time with Mr. Brown but already, Sam's feelings for the older man were growing strong inside him. Mr. Brown opened his eyes and smiled kindly to his young friend.

"I am the only person alive who knows the truth about the Magic Moon Lake. And I cannot let that knowledge die with me."

Sam looked at Mr. Brown more closely. Beneath his deep wrinkles, he had a scar that was slashed across his cheek down to his throat. Sam had never noticed it before.

"Magic Moon Lake? What are you talking about? My family goes swimming in the lake all the time, especially in the summer! But we never *ever* saw or heard anything about this lake being magic."

"Oh, it's a big secret!" Mr. Brown laughed, then cut off when he started coughing. Sam now gave his full attention and listened to every single word that Mr. Brown was saying.

"Sam, I am so thankful that you shot your soccer ball through my window."

"Wow, no one is ever thankful when something bad happens to them," Sam said.

Mr. Brown smiled softly and looked at Sam with the eyes of an understanding father when he said, "*The secret to a happy life is your attitude...* Yes, young warrior, positivity goes a long way. Indeed, I am very thankful that you shot the ball into my window, because if you never had done that, I would not have had the opportunity to tell you the secret of the lake."

"I still don't understand. What do you mean, the lake has a secret? It looks pretty normal to me," Sam mentioned, "unless it has something to do with... Viking ghosts?"

At that moment, Sam heard a shriek overhead. When he looked up, he saw a hawk gliding out of the sky, heading right for the porch! Mr. Brown reached under his chair and quickly put on a long leather glove. He whistled, then called out, "Sagitta!"

Sam couldn't believe his eyes when the hawk swooped right over his head. He ducked and felt the soft brush of feathers on his neck. When he looked up, the magnificent hawk was perched on the glove, on the back of Mr. Brown's forearm. The old man whispered something to the hawk, something in what Sam assumed was a Native American language. Every few words, Sam heard Mr. Brown speak the hawk's name, Sagitta.

Up close, the bird was huge. Her talons looked razor sharp and her beak looked like it could tear apart a bear. Sam's heart pounded as he thought about being this close to such a fierce-looking creature.

But then the bird nuzzled her head into the man's neck. *Like a cat!* Sam thought. It was amazing, actually. This wild creature was cuddling with him!

"Is... is that your pet?" Sam questioned.

The hawk looked over at him and Sam would have sworn she was rolling her eyes. Mr. Brown laughed. "I think it's more the opposite. More like I'm hers."

Sam blinked, trying to understand.

"So now, young warrior, would you like to hear the secret of the Magic Moon Lake?"

CHAPTER TEN

Young Warrior

"This town," Mr. Brown began, "was first settled over one thousand years ago when the Vikings came over from Scandinavia. Norway, to be exact."

Sam's eyes brightened. "So there are Viking ghosts!?" he said, remembering his friend's map and explanation.

"You know," Mr. Brown said, nodding his head. "Apart from my people, not too many know about it."

"Okay," Sam said, his mind whirling, "but how can your people be so sure the Vikings came here?"

Mr. Brown sat up straight. "Who do you think was here ten thousand years before the Vikings? Who do you think met them here? My people!"

The elderly man suddenly looked proud. Dangerous. Wild. Sam realized that, even though Mr. Brown was very old, Sam would not want to cross him.

His mind was spinning. "Wait," he said. "The ruins near the lake. These must be from the Vikings, right?"

Mr. Brown calmed. He smiled and nodded. "Very good."

"The Vikings… hmmm," Sam said, thinking to himself. "Can you tell me more about the story?"

The old man looked up into the sky, once again. A dark look crossed his face, as if he smelled something he didn't like. He turned back to the hawk. Sagitta looked him in the eye, then suddenly took flight. Sam ducked again as the fantastic creature zoomed over his head. The hawk continued to fly out towards the direction of the woods, closer to Moon Lake. Mr. Brown began to hum a melody, then he started chanting words that Sam did not understand. Sam closed his eyes and felt peace in his heart.

Mr. Brown said with his eyes still closed, "The king of the Vikings. His name was Gerald. He was a mighty warrior and he came here with ninety Vikings in three ships. All were heavily armed."

Mr. Brown smiled as he added, "Do you know what the Vikings looked like, Sam?"

"Yeah, mmm kind of… not really," Sam confessed. Mr. Brown was patient and nodded with an understanding look on his face.

"This Viking King, Gerald, had a large helmet with two horns on it. His clothes were of the skin of the brown bear. This Viking king was a powerful man who had won many battles. His army was nearly unstoppable and battle after battle, he continued to succeed. His name was recognized throughout the land and the people praised his name as the undefeated King Gerald. When his reign continued to grow, he commanded his warriors to find a foreign land where he would build a magnificent city."

"I get it. But how does this connect to a secret of Moon Lake?"

"*Patience is bitter, but its fruit is sweet,*" the man said in his sing-song voice, "And Moon Lake is magic! Yes, absolutely magic."

Sam tilted his head back in annoyance and breathed in and out. He wanted to hear the whole story, all at once. "Okay. I'm listening. *Patiently.*" He emphasized.

Mr. Brown continued, unamused, "King Gerald had received word of a well-nourished land in the foreign country across the great sea. Now, he wanted to send Viking families to create his new city and expand his reign. But King Gerald was advised by his wise men that it was time to first unite the kingdom with a Queen on his right hand. Although King Gerald had never lost a battle, Norway was a very violent place and there were many leaders with great armies and even greater ambition. So Gerald needed to find a wife to broaden his control, strengthen his army, and unite the troubled lands.

"King Gerald told his guards to find the ten most beautiful young maidens in all the land and anoint them with oil before his presence. So it happened that they handpicked the most beautiful girls in all of Scandinavia and brought them before the king. King Gerald looked at each of the ten young maidens carefully, but immediately it was obvious. One of them stood out among all the rest. Her beauty was without equal. She was likewise elegant and kind-hearted in nature. A rare woman indeed, as beautiful inside as she was outside. Her name was Aurelia."

Mr. Brown took a sip of water and continued.

"As soon as Gerald saw her, he knew he had to have her as his wife. Gerald commanded this girl to be anointed and made Queen immediately. The beautiful Aurelia was silent when she heard this, because she was scared of Gerald. He was barbaric and his riches did not impress her.

Aurelia was escorted to Gerald's Viking ship. They placed her in royal garments and she waited to be anointed. Aurelia's sadness grew in her heart and finally she began to sob and cry. When the servant girls questioned her about her sadness, she confessed that she was already deeply in love with someone else. King Gerald heard about this and grew very angry."

Sam looked up with wide eyes and asked eagerly, "So what happened?"

Mr. Brown continued, "'No one can tell me no!' Gerald declared. He commanded his guards, 'Bring me the man that Aurelia is in love with so I can speak with him.' King Gerald's warriors quickly discovered that the man she loved already served in King Gerald's army.

The guards returned to Gerald and declared that they had found the man. 'He serves in your army. A brave warrior and a man of good judgment.' When Gerald heard the man's name, he was troubled, for he knew the man. Although he was one of Gerald's best warriors, the king plotted a clever way to get rid of him."

Mr. Brown stopped for a moment to catch his breath. He was getting as worked up as Sam. The old man took three long breaths, in and out.

Sam's eyes were wide open in excitement, but his concern for Mr. Brown grew. "Are you okay?"

"Yes. I'm fine, young warrior. A heavy storm is coming…"

A breeze of cool air passed by as he spoke. The wind chimes that dangled from the roof of the porch gently rang in a sweet melody.

"What!?" Sam jumped up from the floor. "What do you mean a storm is coming? It's clear as can be. Not a cloud in the sky."

Mr. Brown frowned. "Excuse me? Sit back down, son."

Sam immediately sat down. "I don't want to make you angry. I just want to know what happened next." Sam's eyes got watery.

Mr. Brown closed his eyes and began humming again. The sun was beginning to set, and the crickets started singing. Sam waited patiently for a few minutes and folded his hands together, bringing his chin to rest on them. Then Sam asked in a soft voice, "So…"

Mr. Brown looked at Sam and said, "The strongest of all warriors are these two — Time and Patience." Another breeze swept through the garden, leaving Sam speechless.

"And I believe your mother is here to pick you up."

Sam leapt off the porch and looked down the driveway. The entrance was clearly empty, and he didn't see anyone.

"Mr. Brown, I think you're mistaken. She isn't here."

"Look again, young warrior."

At that moment, Sam's mother pulled into the driveway. She hit the car horn in two quick beeps.

Sam's mouth fell open. "Wait. What? How?" Mr. Brown looked back up at the sky and began humming again.

"But what happened next?" Sam pleaded. "What do the Vikings have to do with the lake? You can't just end the story on me like that."

Mr. Brown slowly nodded. "Monday, after school, you can come back and hear the rest of the story."

"Awesome! I'll see you Monday then, Mr. Brown! Thanks for everything!"

Sam leaned over and gave the man a hug, taking him by surprise. Mr. Brown smiled and held Sam tight for a moment.

"Sounds good, young warrior," he said.

Sam pulled away from the hug. "I never got to ask, but why do you call me that?"

Mr. Brown suddenly grew very serious. His eyes flashed.

"There is something coming. Something dark and dangerous. I don't know exactly what it is yet, but I feel it has something to do with you."

Sam felt a shiver run down his spine. "But I'm not a warrior."

Mr. Brown tightened his lips. "I'm afraid that, like it or not, soon you will have to be."

CHAPTER ELEVEN

A Storm is Coming

BOOM! Thunder shook the skies. Sam ran to the living room window. Heavy rain started pouring onto the sidewalks in a consistent rhythm. Lightning flickered in the distance.

"Come on, Sam," his father called from the couch, the TV remote in his hand. "The movie's about to start."

His mother was pouring hot tea into four cups. More and more these days, Leah was finding excuses not to share movie night with the family. This time she was there though, even if her eyes were glued to her cell phone as she texted furiously. Sam wasn't very excited to see the romantic comedy and suspected his parents had chosen it to lure Leah back to movie night.

The aroma of hot tea seemed to warm the whole living room, but outside the weather was no joke. Sam blinked as a bright flash of lightning lit the sky somewhere far behind Alex's house. He only got as far as counting to "three-one-thousand" in his head before the loud crash of thunder shook the house. Even Leah looked up from her cell phone—for a moment.

As Sam continued to gaze into the darkness through the window, he saw that the rain had created thin rivers along both borders of his street.

The trees swayed heavily back and forth in the strong wind. Mr. Brown had warned him that a storm was coming. Sam had thought he was being mysterious and metaphorical. But here it was, a real storm. Sam's mind, in fact, hadn't been able to stop whirling over what Mr. Brown had told him earlier that day.

What exactly did the Vikings have to do with Moon Lake? Sam wondered, staring past his own reflection in the window at the downpour. *And then there's Alex and all his talk about ghosts.* It had sounded crazy when he mentioned it but now that Mr. Brown started talking about Vikings... and magic...

I don't believe in ghosts, Sam thought.

Then he squinted into the darkness. *Do I?*

Sam rubbed his eyes. It was all very confusing. Vikings, ghosts, screeching sounds coming from the lake, and most mysterious of all — the medallion.

A week ago, Sam would have laughed at the idea of ghosts haunting Moon Lake. But now, after all he had gone through with falling in the water and finding the mystical medallion? He couldn't be sure of anything.

FLASH! A stunning burst of lightning blinded Sam, immediately followed by a crash of thunder that was so loud, Sam felt it in his bones. The floor beneath him shook. The lights and TV shut off instantly, leaving the Lawrence's in pitch darkness. For a moment, everyone held their breath. In the blackness, Sam could hear the living room chandelier tinkling as it was apparently swaying from the concussion.

"Oh my," Mrs. Lawrence gasped.

"Nothing to worry about," Mr. Lawrence assured her. "Everyone stay put." Sam heard his father stand up from the couch and walk across the room.

"I think it hit right outside!" Sam said, turning back to look out the window. "The streetlights are out."

"Take it easy, munchkin," Leah sighed. "It's just a little lightning."

"I know that!" Sam shot back. "Looks like you won't be able to see your corny romantic movie after all."

A beam of light pierced the darkness. Sam's dad had pulled the flashlight out of his sheriff's utility belt that always hung near the front door when he was home. Mrs. Lawrence struck a match and started lighting the living room candles that, until now, had only been decorations.

Mr. Lawrence stepped over to Sam and peered out the window. "The whole street is out. No sense flipping the breaker. Hopefully it's just the transformer down the street. I'll call in just to be sure."

Sam's dad picked up his cell phone off the coffee table and stepped into the kitchen.

"It's getting late anyway," Mrs. Lawrence said. "Perhaps we should go to bed. We have church in the morning."

Reluctantly, Sam followed Leah up the stairs, each of them carrying a candle. Sam went into his room, shut the door, and placed the candle on his desk.

The dim light of the flame flickered softly, casting long shadows on his walls as thunder continued to rumble through the neighborhood. Geezer jumped on Sam's bed, meowing loudly.

"It's okay, Geezer. Just a storm." Sam scratched his cat's ears.

Sam was starting to take off his shirt and get ready for bed when he heard a car door slam. It sounded close, like it came from across the street.

Thinking quickly, Sam blew out his candle and inched toward the window. Through the rivulets of rainwater streaming down the glass, Sam looked across the street and saw a flashlight beam swinging back and forth outside the Fisher's house. Sam blinked at it, trying to see who was carrying it.

Just then, the beam swung wildly, washing right over Sam's window. Sam quickly pulled away, falling on his back.

The beam of light penetrated his room and swung this way and that, as if searching for him. He gulped and flattened himself on the floor, his heart beating faster.

And then suddenly, as if giving up, the flashlight beam swung away.

Carefully, Sam crept over to the window and slowly raised his head up to look outside. The flashlight was now perched on top of Mr. Fisher's car in the driveway, aimed into the Fisher's front yard. Sam squinted into the dim light.

There... A shape. A man. Bent over and pulling something.

A scratching sound reached Sam's ears from across the street. Whoever the person was, he was dragging something big and heavy.

Just as Sam wondered who the person was and what they were doing, the figure backed into the flashlight's beam. It was Mr. Fisher, looking more like a mad scientist than ever before. Although the rain was pouring down, he was wearing a bathrobe and slippers. Gusts of wind blew his hair in all directions. For a moment, it struck Sam that Alex's father looked like he had just escaped from a mental hospital. As if sensing Sam's presence, Mr. Fisher spun his head around to look into Sam's window.

Sam dropped to the floor again and held his breath. A few seconds ticked by. Then Sam heard the scratching sound again and poked his head back up.

There, in the rain, Mr. Fisher struggled to haul a large box wrapped in a dark cloth. From what Sam could see, it must have been very heavy.

The cloth seemed to get stuck on a rock in the driveway. When Mr. Fisher yanked at it, the dark cloth rose up about a foot off the ground on one side of the box. Staring through the rain, Sam caught sight of a silvery reflection.

Wait, Sam thought, squinting, *are those — metal bars?*

Just as Mr. Fisher rushed to pull the cloth down and recover the box, Sam realized that it wasn't completely solid. It was made of silver poles. Like...

A cage? Is that thing a big cage?!

Mr. Fisher rubbed at his back, then continued hauling the box. Finally, he got it into the house. One last time, Mr. Fisher looked around the neighborhood nervously and slammed the front door shut.

Sam felt uneasy spying like this, but Mr. Fisher had been acting so suspicious. He clenched his eyebrows together, wondering.

The rain started letting up. Soft droplets pattered on the window as the downpour now became a light drizzle.

Sam shook his head and felt a shiver, genuinely spooked. He sat on his bed and started petting Geezer, absent-mindedly. The cat purred, unbothered.

"Was that thing really a big cage?" Sam whispered to Geezer.

Purring proudly, Geezer nodded his head as if in agreement.

"I've always thought Mr. Fisher was a little creepy, but this is evidence that he's up to something. I wonder if Alex is telling me everything. I wonder if it has to do with Moon Lake."

Sam walked to his desk and opened the drawer.

"Something isn't right in Moon Lake," he said down into the soft glow of the medallion. Sam's pupils grew bigger, darker. He straightened himself up.

"And I need to find out what it is."

Sam reached into the drawer and pulled out the medallion. He held it up to the candlestick so he could inspect it carefully. Even though he'd looked at the medallion many times before, he felt compelled to look at it closer right now. Maybe he had missed something before. The turquoise color of the stone at the medallion's center seemed deeper and darker than before. The intricate design etched into the stone looked like a maze of uncharted waters. As Sam held it closer and closer to the flame, the pattern in the center of the medallion's stone slowly began to move.

Sam gasped. He couldn't believe what he was seeing. Maybe it was lightning that tricked his eyes. He looked again.

No. It wasn't lightning. It was the medallion itself.

Its stone was swirling, breathing. Its maze design was slowly morphing from one pattern to another, looking almost like a slow-moving storm system. Sam gazed at it, unblinking, his mouth hanging open just a little.

It was mesmerizing, hypnotizing, but in a warm and comforting way. Sam couldn't take his eyes off of it. He noticed strange markings on the side of the medallion. He'd never noticed them before.

As he rubbed the medallion with his thumb, a sudden flash of green light burst from its center, straight into Sam's pupils—and then disappeared just as quickly.

Sam held his breath.

His eyes widened. *Did that just happen?*

Sam whispered to himself, "This medallion came from the lake."

He clutched the amulet in his fists and it was like he felt a strong urge take over his entire body. He was fearless.

"I must find out why the medallion was at the lake in the first place, and what it's trying to tell me now!"

CHAPTER TWELVE

The Lady in the Water

Sam had never before snuck out of the house at night. But he didn't give it a second thought. His father had left for the office to lend a hand to any in need during the storm. Leah and his mother were asleep. Sam crept through the dark house, quietly opened the garage door only as high as he needed, grabbed his bike, and then closed the door behind him, silently.

Thankfully, the rain had stopped, though Sam would've left even in the thick of the storm. No matter what, Sam was going to find out what mission the medallion had sent him on. He pedaled quickly, ignoring how the wet road made his bike slip and slide.

He pedaled faster and faster, feeling the need to get to the lake as quickly as possible, his heart pounding so hard it felt like it was going to burst out of his chest. With the medallion in his pocket, he didn't even feel how ice cold the air was. He simply felt powerful. Energized.

Finally reaching the path next to the twins' house, he walked his bike into the forest a little ways and hid it behind a clump of pine trees. The breeze pushed the tall trees back and forth, making them creak eerily.

Determined, nonetheless, he veered off the normal path and began marching down a less traveled, overgrown trail that Sam and Ethan had found the previous summer. They had used the path just a few times, to get to a remote part of the lake, about a quarter of the way around, where they had set up a rope swing. This time Sam walked right past the swing, the bottom of his jeans getting soaked from the wet grass.

This was the first time that Sam went so far down the trail. Past the rope swing, the trail became harder and harder to see. Bushes and trees grew so thick that Sam felt like he was making his way through a jungle. Surely no one had used this old trail in many years. And why would they? There was really no reason to go to the overgrown side of the lake — the "creepy side" as Ethan called it.

Sam pushed his way through prickly bushes and soon realized he was staring at the old boathouse. His hands were covered in scratches and his sneakers were filled with water, but he had made it to the other side. He was back where he had originally found the medallion.

Sam walked through the fallen logs and squishy moss until he was at the water's edge. Staring out into the distance, he focused on the lake, looking for anything out of the ordinary. Maybe an animal, some kind of fish, ripples—or even a ghost. But there was nothing. Only the unique chorus of crickets and frogs.

Fog crept over the surface of the water, glowing from the light of the slowly emerging moonlight as it crept out from behind the dissipating rain clouds.

"What's everyone afraid of?" Sam said out loud. "Ghosts? Ha." He let out a defeated laugh. "There's nothing here."

Sam inched over to an area of bare sand and sat down. He closed his eyes and let himself be lulled into a meditative state by the music of the frog and cricket choir.

He waited…

And waited…

And waited some more.

"I knew it," Sam finally said to no one in particular. "There's no secret here. Just a made-up legend. Mr. Brown was just trying to get me to listen some of his old legends. And Mr. Fisher, well, he's just off his rocker."

Sam stood up with a huff. He grabbed a flat stone off the ground and heaved it, sidearm, toward the lake. The thin rock skipped four times until it sank. The ripples spread silently across the glassy surface, interrupted here and there by floating leaves and half-submerged branches.

Wait, the pattern, he realized — *I've seen it before.*

Sam took the medallion from his pocket. The center stone was glowing green and yes — the pattern in its etchings was exactly the same as the ripple pattern on the lake. Sam shuddered.

Suddenly everything was quiet. No crickets chirping. No frogs croaking. No far off thunder. Even the trees seemed to stop rustling. Unexpectedly, the moon ducked behind the only cloud left in the sky, and the lake went pitch black. Chills crept down Sam's spine.

Then, out on the lake, he heard a splash.

He didn't move a muscle as he scanned the center of the lake with wide eyes. His body stiffened. He could hear his heartbeat pounding in his ears.

Who's… there? Sam thought, swallowing hard.

Out in the center of the lake, something was happening. The water started to churn in one specific spot. Ripples branched out from it. Now the water was bubbling and almost seemed to boil.

A bright blue and green beam of light shot up from the roiling water, heading straight up into the sky. Sam involuntarily jumped back a few feet.

"What in the world?" Sam's breathing quickened.

The wind flared up, lifting a million droplets of water up into the air. Very quickly it looked as if a tiny water spout was spinning over the bubbling water, revolving around the beam of light. Real waves now, not just ripples, exploded from a miniature storm funnel.

The colorful beam started to pulse—soft then bright. The pulsing gained momentum, faster and faster, brighter and brighter. It was the most mesmerizing thing Sam had ever seen—until what happened next.

As Sam stood, gaping at the sight, two delicate hands slowly rose from the water, right in the middle of the spectacle. They turned elegantly, slowly rotating in the water, like two dancers entwining round each other.

Whatever—or whoever—was in the water was rising, slowly. Two graceful forearms followed the hands. The arms glowed in a soft, soothing blue-green color.

Next, a head adorned with long, silver flowing hair rose from the water with its back to Sam. Sam found himself leaning to the side to try and get a look at the figure's face. The figure continued rising upwards and a young woman's torso emerged. Slender and elegant, she kept her hands pointed up toward the sky. Water dripped down her arms, off her body, and slid effortlessly back into the lake. Still, Sam could only see her back and he yearned to see her from the front. At that moment, an eerie, piercing sound shot across the lake, filling Sam's ears.

His blood froze.

The grating, high-pitched sound was gruesome and completely out of place with the beautiful scene before Sam's eyes. The woman continued to swirl her arms and hands towards the sky, but the terrible shrill sound grew louder. As if in tune with it, the medallion in Sam's hands began to vibrate. Sam felt it pulling his hands toward the center of the lake, like it was magnetized to the woman and longed to be with her.

Instinctively, he wrapped his hands around it tightly, pulling it back toward his chest. Still, he could feel it tugging at his hands to be free. On impulse, Sam placed the medallion around his neck. The second he did, the macabre sound from the lake disappeared.

In its place, Sam suddenly heard a beautiful sound. He cocked his head. It sounded like—humming? Yes. Strange as it seemed, where a moment ago there had been that shrill sound, like nails down a chalkboard, now instead Sam heard the young woman in the lake humming a sweet tune. The melody of the song and the quality of her voice were so exquisite, Sam didn't ever want it to stop. He felt his body leaning toward it, drawn to it. It was the most enchanting sound he had ever heard. He watched in awe as the mystical young woman moved her hands in sync with her melody. From where Sam stood, facing her back, he could see what looked like a bikini strap across her back made out of what seemed to be seaweed or water grass. Her long hair shone silver-blue in the moonlight, swaying as if in slow motion, glistening like pale, liquid fire.

Just as Sam thought he could stand there and listen to the sound forever, the humming stopped. Sam felt his body deflate in disappointment, yearning to hear it again. But just then the young woman stopped twirling and turned around to face Sam.

Sam's mouth dropped open.

She was the most beautiful girl he had ever seen.

The young woman seemed to be about sixteen years old. Her skin was silvery and glowed with an inner light. As he stood there staring speechless, the young woman smiled at him.

It was too much. Sam felt overcome. Powerless and weak. The world started spinning, then everything went black. Sam's legs gave out and he dropped to the ground, unconscious.

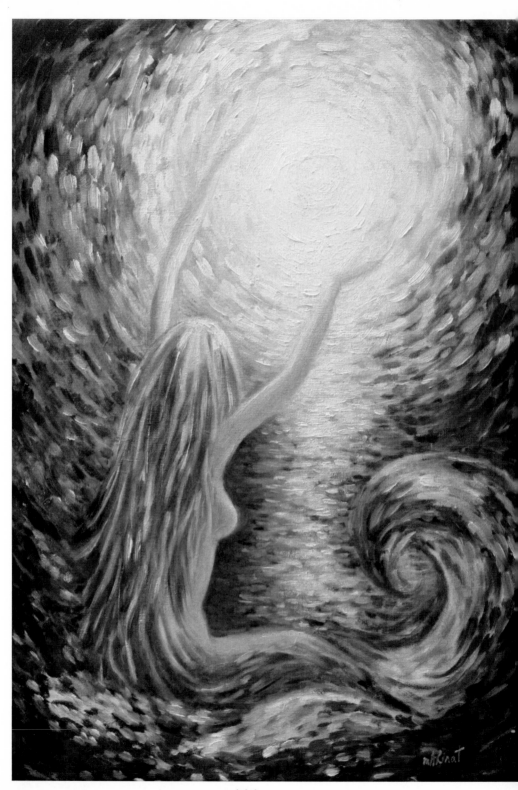

CHAPTER THIRTEEN

Aurelia

Sam was falling. And falling. Like he would never touch the Earth again. Something was following him, chasing him. He couldn't see it since everything was pitch black, but he felt its presence. And it was getting closer. Gaining on him. Sam opened his mouth to scream, but no sound came out. He clenched his fists, swallowed hard, and tried with every fiber of his being to yell. As he opened his mouth, he came rushing back to consciousness.

Sam saw stars above. He was lying on his back, he realized. He was at the water's edge. It was all just a dream. He took a deep breath. Nothing was chasing him. He was safe.

Now why am I here again? Sam wondered. *The lake. Why am I at the lake...* Then a face leaned over him and Sam screamed for real.

Now he remembered. The young woman in the lake. *Wait,* Sam thought. *Is she... is this...?*

"You're real?" Sam finally croaked. The young woman giggled. It was a beautiful, delicate sound, like tiny wind chimes made of diamonds.

"Of course I'm real, silly," she said. Then she frowned. "Are you all right? Can you sit up?"

She gazed deeply into Sam's eyes. His heart almost stopped as he looked at her. She blinked at him and his heart nearly broke with how it made him feel. Her skin had a faint turquoise tint. Surrounding her fragile features was her wavy, silver hair, plunging over her shoulders. A pair of arched eyebrows floated atop sweeping eyelashes. But Sam couldn't stop staring at her eyes. They were a captivating shade of deep emerald and actually seemed to be glowing the same colors as the medallion. Sam had never seen a girl so beautiful in his life. She smiled down at him, as if she knew exactly the effect she was having on him.

"I felt your presence," she said in her melodious tone. "What brings you here?"

"I-I-I," Sam stuttered. He wasn't sure what to say. He was still in shock.

Again, she giggled. Sam's stomach turned to butterflies.

He wanted to talk but was afraid he would break some kind of spell and make the young woman disappear. And he didn't want to let that to happen. Ever.

"Here," she said, "sit up."

Her touch was cold, but Sam didn't care. He felt her fingers on his arm, pulling him up off his back.

Sitting up, Sam noticed that the young woman was lying halfway on the shore, propped up on her elbows. The bottom half of her was still in the lake. Sam looked down at his arm and saw that her long, pointed fingernails were blue. Then his eyes widened as he noticed the thin webbing between her fingers.

Sam's eyes traced the ground over to her waist. As he looked closer he could see now that, from the waist down, the woman had the shape of a fish, covered with shimmering silver-blue scales and a fluke.

"You're a…" he said as he lost his words.

He had visited the lake hoping that he might glimpse something supernatural, maybe even a ghost, but to actually see what was in front of him right now — it was something else entirely.

She smiled, tenderly. "A mermaid. Yes I am."

"It's a dream," Sam said. "It must be."

She smiled. "You humans used to believe in legends. What happened to you?"

"I do believe — I mean, I came here to —" Sam couldn't finish. He was staring at her bikini top. Then he turned away, his face reddening.

"Um. So. How old are you?" he asked nervously.

She answered without equivocation, "Three hundred this year."

"Really?" he asked. "You don't look a day over sixteen."

She smiled. "I am Aurelia. Tell me your name." The mermaid's voice was cool and fresh like bubbles rising out of the ocean.

"Uh… my name is Sam. I heard about you through a legend…" Sam stuttered, rather shyly.

"A legend?" the mermaid asked as she put her arms over one another and rested her chin on them. When she closed and opened her eyes, the way her eyelashes moved made Sam feel calm and relaxed.

She was sitting right in front of him and still his heart ached for her. Like he craved being near her—when he already was. Aurelia's face filled with curiosity. She started playing with a tiny strand of her wavy hair.

"Yes, I heard about you," Sam said. "But I thought you were some kind of a Viking ghost… not a mermaid."

"Oh, Viking ghosts?" the mermaid said in mock surprise. Then she laughed and continued to gaze at Sam with her hypnotizing green eyes.

"Yes," Sam said as he swallowed a lump in his throat, "I mean, I knew the lake had something to do with the legend of the Vikings."

"Tell me about these Vikings that you speak of." Aurelia said sweetly.

Sam cleared his throat once more, "I know that the Vikings took you away. And that King Gerald wanted to make you his wife."

"Stop!" The mermaid Aurelia demanded. Her eyes flashed fiercely. She lifted her tail high above the water.

Sam involuntarily jumped up and stepped backwards, suddenly afraid.

"Wh-what?" Sam asked, shivering. "What did I do wrong?"

"Don't ever speak that name again," the mermaid declared, then slammed her luminous tail back into the water with a loud splash.

Cold water rained down on Sam, sending an icy sensation down his spine.

The lake went suddenly quiet. Just as before, not a single sound came from either side of the forest. Sam's heart beat like a freight train. Seconds ticked by. Then the lonely "ooooh" of an owl floated softly through the distance.

Sam stuttered, "Oh, I'm sorry. I just –I…"

"I know," The mermaid said gently. "Sam, you must understand that the king did such a bad thing to me. You wouldn't want to imagine what happened."

The mermaid started to weep, with tears rolling down her face.

"Oh no," Sam said. Seeing her cry felt like a needle stabbing his heart.

He wanted to comfort her more than anything he had ever wanted before. She was still halfway in the water. Sam walked back to her, sat down cross-legged, and reached over to hold her hand. He was sitting in wet mud and again her skin felt cold to the touch, but Sam didn't care about any of that.

"Don't cry…" Sam comforted her.

The beautiful mermaid leaned over and rested her head on Sam's shoulder. An electric tingle raced through his body.

"Oh Sam, it's been so long since I've had a real friend," the mermaid said with a sad smile. "I wasn't always a fish woman, you know?" A small, pathetic sob escaped her lips.

"What happened?" Sam asked. Without meaning to, he started running his fingers through her sparkling, silver hair.

"The Viking witch did this to me," Aurelia said, "She tricked me. She placed me in this wretched pool of water and left me without my love."

Sam was silent as he tried to understand her words. *Ghosts. Mermaids. Witches.* It was a lot to process. Sam watched as the moonlight reflected on the water like a shimmery, silver path.

The fog had returned, denser than before. Suddenly Aurelia turned her head to look directly up at Sam. She sniffled and looked deeply into Sam's eyes, as if looking into his soul. He felt her sadness. It was as if whatever she felt, he felt.

"Sam," she breathed, "I'm trapped here. I need your help."

"Please," he whispered back. "Don't be so sad. Something as beautiful as you should never be so sad."

Aurelia gave him a small, heart-wrenching smile. "You're very kind. I have no friend here; I have no one to help me."

"Well... maybe I can help you," Sam suggested.

Aurelia's eyes brightened. Quickly, she sat up straight. With a blush, Sam wished she hadn't moved her head from his lap. He felt comfortable with her in his arms.

"Would you?" Aurelia said, blinking like an eager child.

"What can I do?" Sam asked. "Anything. I'll do whatever I can to help."

Aurelia reached out to clasp both of Sam's hands. "I can't believe how lucky I am to have found you!"

"Come," Aurelia said excitedly, "I want to show you something!" Still holding Sam's hands, she inched herself back toward the icy water, pulling him with her, all the while keeping her gaze on him. Sam tensed, holding back.

"What's wrong?" Aurelia asked, confused.

Looking at the water skeptically, Sam asked, "Where do you want to take me?"

"You'll see! Just come with me, underwater," the mermaid replied.

"Underwater?" Sam gulped. "Uh, so you mean I have to swim with you in the lake?"

"Yes, silly," Aurelia giggled, splashing her beautiful tail in excitement. "How else would you go?"

"But Aurelia, I, uh," Sam scratched his head. "I don't know how else to say it. But I can't breathe underwater like you can."

Aurelia squeezed his hands. "Oh don't worry about that. Come on! It's an amazing sight," she gushed. "Completely indescribable."

Aurelia moved back toward Sam, stretching out so that her face was only a few inches from his. She stared into his eyes. "I've never shown it to anyone, but I trust you."

Sam swelled with pride when she told him that. Now that she was so close, he found himself speechless. Her beauty was breathtaking.

"Don't you trust me?" Aurelia asked with a sweet pout and a flicker of her eyelashes.

"Sure, sure I do," Sam said quickly. "But..."

"But?" Aurelia's eyes flashed. "But, but, but!" she said, raising her voice. "You don't trust me, do you? Fine."

Aurelia shoved herself backwards and disappeared completely into the lake with a splash.

"Wait!" Sam shouted. "Hey!"

Aurelia's head popped out of the water. Moonlight danced in her silvery hair. Her glowing, green eyes bore into Sam.

"You said you were going to help me," she said flatly. "I thought I could trust you." Then she disappeared back into the lake.

"Aurelia!" he called. "Come back!"

Sam scanned the water for any sign of her, but there was none. No ripple, no splash, no sign of her sparkling, silvery hair.

He listened hard. But all he could hear was the crickets and frogs.

"No, no, no," Sam whispered to himself, harshly. "You idiot! Why did you do that? Aurelia?"

Sam knew that if he never saw her again, he would regret it for the rest of his life.

"Darn it!" he said. "Aurelia! Wait!"

Sam kicked off his shoes then ripped off his socks, shirt and pants. A gust of wind came through the trees. In his boxer shorts, Sam shivered. Goose bumps prickled his arms. He realized how cold it was and how cold the lake water looked.

"This is crazy," Sam said, hugging himself.

The fog drifted over the water. Steam rose up from the lake.

Sam took a deep breath and blew it out, loudly. Then he ran into the water, waving his hands in the air. "Aurelia! Wait! I want to go with you."

He waded into the water until he couldn't touch the bottom. Then he swam out towards the center of the lake. The clouds of his breath merged with the thickening fog covering the calm surface.

Sam quickly grew tired and stopped swimming. Not a single ripple erupted from the lake's surface.

The fog gathered around Sam like a white blanket. He looked around and grew frightened. He could no longer see the shoreline.

"Aurelia!" Sam shouted, splashing his hands in the water. But the mermaid was nowhere in sight. The dense fog surrounding Sam grew even thicker. Clouds started passing by the moon and suddenly Sam was plunged into total darkness.

What am I doing here? Sam did not understand in which direction to swim. And he was growing more and more tired, treading water. He beat the water with his fists in frustration.

Then Sam noticed a dim green light below him through the murky water. The light appeared to be coming closer to him.

"Aurelia?" he called into the water. "Is that you?"

Suddenly, something gripped his foot. Something strong. Sam gasped. He barely had time to gulp a big breath of air before whatever it was, tugged him under.

CHAPTER FOURTEEN

Submerged

Underwater, Sam instinctively screamed, letting go of all the air in his lungs. He squirmed and kicked, trying to reach the water's surface. Then he opened his eyes and saw the mermaid right in front of him. Aurelia's tail was glowing bright green and blue, illuminating all the surrounding water. Sam was stunned in awe. Her long, silver hair spread out all around her head. It was incredible but somehow, underwater, she was even more beautiful than on land.

Aurelia smiled and grabbed Sam around the waist. She was surprisingly strong. Aurelia reached out and stroked his cheek. Sam let out the last bit of bubbles from his chest and pointed to his mouth, then the surface, trying to tell her that he needed air, desperately. But Aurelia held him tight as he slowly stopped struggling. He felt his heart pound in his chest and wondered if this was it; the last moment of his life.

Aurelia's face floated close to Sam's. Even so near to death, her beauty overcame him. Calmly, the mermaid blinked at him, fluttering her eyelashes.

And then she kissed him.

Sam's eyes grew wide in shock. They both merged their lips, half open. Her lips were so soft. Sam could feel strands of her hair brushing his face. He felt her chest press into his.

The kiss was timeless, endless. Magical.

Suddenly, Sam felt a huge burst of air enter his mouth and shoot down into his lungs. It happened fast.

Wait a second. What just happened? Sam thought. *My first kiss… to a mermaid?* Sam opened his eyes.

Aurelia pulled back, smiling at him. Then she nodded. She pointed to his mouth, then his chest.

Sam felt funny. He blew bubbles of air out his nose. Though he was underwater with his mouth closed, his lungs inflated and Sam felt like he had just taken a big breath of air. He blew more bubbles. Then he pumped up his lungs again. It was amazing. It was just as if he was above the water, breathing. Every time he puffed up his chest, somehow he got another lungful of air.

I can breathe underwater!

Sam looked around. He could see much more detail underwater now. The lake wasn't nearly as murky as it had been a second ago.

And my vision is clearer, Sam thought. *Magic!*

The sound of Aurelia's giggle met Sam's ears—just as clear as it had been on the shore. Somehow the mermaid's magic kiss had transformed him. He didn't need air. And now he could see and hear underwater better than any human should.

It was amazing!

Aurelia's silver hair floated around her face, glowing with the reflection of colors from her tail. Just looking at her, made Sam feel like he was melting. He felt a strong connection towards Aurelia. It was something he had never felt before. Looking at her in all her underwater majesty, tiny bits of electricity filled his body and exploded like fireworks. Sam felt warm and secure with Aurelia beside him.

Aurelia pulled him to her and hugged him. She twirled herself around him and spun them both round and round, pulling him tighter to her. Sam hugged the mermaid back and felt himself in complete bliss. He wanted to kiss her again. And again.

Aurelia pulled back as she saw the necklace Sam was wearing. It was the medallion. She smiled and then touched it with her index finger. The medallion immediately began to glow brightly, pulsing with the exact same colors as Aurelia's tail. Against his chest, Sam felt the medallion vibrating with warmth, almost as if it were alive.

Aurelia grabbed Sam's hand and gave a kick of her tail. The two of them took off like an arrow, racing underwater. Sam gripped her hand tighter and felt the smile spread across his face. It was exhilarating! They were going so fast! Fish darted out of their way. Aurelia angled them downward and pulled them deeper into the lake.

As they descended, Sam noticed that the deeper they went, the more he could see. The medallion and Aurelia's tail lit up everything surrounding them. Soon enough, they came to the bottom of the lake. It was covered in sand, small rocks, and wavy water plants.

Aurelia brought Sam to a small hole in the bottom of the lake hidden by tall rocks and seaweed. It was too narrow for them to enter side by side so Aurelia swam through first, then waved back to Sam.

He followed her without a moment of hesitation. Sam found himself in a tight tunnel, only a bit wider than his own body. He kicked with his legs and used his hands to grip the sides of the rock tunnel and pull himself forward.

After just a minute, the tunnel opened up and Sam found himself in a huge underwater cavern.

He couldn't believe his eyes. It was massive, about as long and wide as a football field. Sam could see a soft light overhead, maybe thirty or forty feet above. The smooth rock walls around him were glowing in different hues of purple, blue and green.

The colors pulsed slowly, swaying with the gentle water current. Embedded in the rocks were tiny gleaming crystals that reflected the lights from the mermaid's tail and Sam's medallion.

Aurelia waited for him, admiring his awestruck look of the size and beauty of the underwater cavern. She took his hand again and with just a few swishes of the massive fluke of her tail, pushed them upwards. Fish of all sizes and types swam by them.

Quickly, the two reached the surface. Sam burst through the top of the water, gasped, and felt fresh air rush into his lungs. Sam pulled himself up onto the dry rocks surrounding the surface of the water and sat down.

Around him was a sparkling, colorful cave. The space seemed larger than his whole house, and taller too. The same colorful rock walls that he had seen under the water continued up into the cave as well, meeting in the high ceiling that glittered with more reflective crystals. Every color of the rainbow shone softly back at Sam. There was no natural light in the cave, but a fire was burning off to the side.

Aurelia pulled herself out of the water next to Sam and reclined onto a soft seaweed bed. She stretched out her beautiful green and blue tail and shook the water drops off of it.

"See Sam? When you trust in me, beautiful things can happen."

The mermaid's voice echoed throughout the walls of the cave melodically.

Sam couldn't help but inch himself even closer to the mermaid. The air was thick and humid and had a sort of rotten seaweed smell to it, but Sam quickly got used to it. He could hear a faint dripping noise echoing as droplets of condensation slid off the rocks and into the pool.

"What is this place?" Sam asked.

"This is where I live," Aurelia said. "Do you like it?"

"I love it!"

Aurelia laughed as Sam's exclamation echoed off the walls.

"Wow," Sam said in awe. "I had no idea there was a cave like this under the water. Moon Lake looks so ordinary from the surface."

"You can never judge something by what's on the surface," Aurelia said seriously.

But Sam was gazing around the cave in astonishment. Glistening stalactites and stalagmites of rock hung from the ceiling and sprouted the ground. Sam peered into a darker corner of the cave and then recognized something.

"Hey, no way," he said, jumping up. "Is that what I think it is?"

Aurelia smiled and slid back into the water.

In a moment, she popped up near the darker corner and pulled herself onto the sandy beach there.

"Come," she beckoned. "Bring a torch."

Sam pulled a burning branch from the fire and walked toward his new friend—and toward what was probably the most curious sight he had ever seen.

CHAPTER FIFTEEN

The Mermaid's Tale

"I can't believe it. A real Viking ship?"

Aurelia nodded. It was true. There leaning against one side of the huge cave was a wooden ship. It looked hundreds of years old and some of it was rotting away. But it was complete with oars, a broken mast, even a tattered sail. Sam gasped as he looked down. Surrounding the ship were thousands of jewels and gold coins.

"This is my collection," Aurelia breathed.

"It must be worth a fortune!" Sam said. "How did you get that ship here?"

Aurelia sighed. "The river that connects the lake to the sea used to be a lot bigger. So big that the Vikings sailed with their entire fleet of ships straight up the river to Moon Lake."

"What happened to the Vikings?"

Aurelia waved her hand as if brushing away a fly. Then she reached into the water and quickly grabbed a tiny fish. With one gulp she swallowed it whole. Sam flinched.

"Let's talk about you, Sam. Tell me about the life you live on land. Do you have a family?"

"My family is alright, I guess" Sam said with a shrug. "My mom, dad, sister, and my pet cat, Geezer."

"You have a sister?" Aurelia perked up and sat a little straighter. "What's her name?"

"Leah," Sam explained. "She's seventeen years old."

"Oh, she must be so pretty!" Aurelia said as she pulled her tail up onto the sand. "Because, you know, you're so handsome."

"I guess you could say that," Sam blushed and croaked with a nervous laugh. "In school, all the boys like her."

"Does she come to the lake? Like you?" Aurelia laid her fingers on Sam's arm.

Though the mermaid was cold, Sam's skin tingled wonderfully at the touch.

"Yeah. Sometimes," Sam shrugged. "Actually, her friend Julia was talking about a lake party happening this week."

Aurelia raised her eyebrows as she turned her gaze to the gemstone on Sam's neck. She reached out and wrapped her long blue fingernails around the medallion. Then she started rubbing the center stone with her thumb. Sam noticed again the thin bluish webbing that connected each of her fingers.

"I'm happy you found my medallion," Aurelia said.

"Why?" Sam asked.

"You know, this medallion is special. It sometimes has a mind of its own. Although, it sometimes misbehaves, it can be calmed when it has a master who can tell it what to do…"

For a moment, Sam felt uneasy. But then Aurelia lifted her eyes back to Sam and added, "Luckily, it was good this time and my little medallion brought you to me."

Patterns seemed to swirl inside her shimmering pupils, like the ones Sam had seen in the medallion's center stone. Sam felt calm, warm, and comfortable. In fact, he had never felt so relaxed or agreeable.

A soft sob escaped Aurelia's lips. She splashed her tail fluke into the water.

"What's wrong, Aurelia?" Sam asked, upset with himself for somehow causing the mermaid distress. Sam reached for her hand and moved closer to her at the edge of the sand.

After a moment, she wiped her tears away with the back of her hand and again rested her head in Sam's lap, looking up at him. Aurelia's pale, silver hair plunged over her shoulders and seaweed top.

"I feel like my life has been taken away from me," Aurelia explained as she fought another sob.

"Why do you say that?"

"It's a long story," the mermaid said. Her voice trailed off in sadness. Sam tightened his lips. He wiped away a few tears from Aurelia's cheeks.

"It has to do with..." Sam stopped, remembering he shouldn't mention the Viking king's name. "He wanted to make you his wife, right? But you refused."

"Yes. I did. I would never wish to be his wife! He was so aggressive, barbaric and cruel to his people." Aurelia frowned.

"After he took me away from my family in Scandinavia and put me on his ship, I tried to think of any way to escape him. But they constantly watched me."

Aurelia started crying again, shaking with sobs. Sam leaned down and wrapped his arms around her, as if he could shield her from everything bad in the world.

"Please don't cry. It'll be okay." Slowly, Aurelia grew silent. She looked down at her tail and breathed deeply. Each of her scales glowed bright with green and blue tones.

"The medicine woman did this to me. That witch. She tricked me. I thought the medicine woman was my friend. She knew that I was already in love with someone else... Kristian." Aurelia sighed.

"The medicine woman told me she would help me escape. I believed her. But people are not always what they seem on the outside. Words can be deceiving."

Aurelia's sad voice echoed around the cave as she paused, taking a deep breath as if on the edge of something very painful.

"The medicine woman told me the only way I could disappear from the king forever would be to submerge myself in the lake, in the moonlight. She gave me the medallion you are wearing now and told me to come, alone, that same night, during the full moon. If I put the medallion around my neck, she said, and submerged myself underwater, I would become invisible to the king and his men. To everyone but Kristian, she said. She gave me the medallion and rubbed my legs with an ointment while she chanted in a strange language."

Aurelia looked down as she caressed her mermaid tail. Her icy blue fingernails slowly traced the scales. Each scale shimmered with a bioluminescence glow as she touched it.

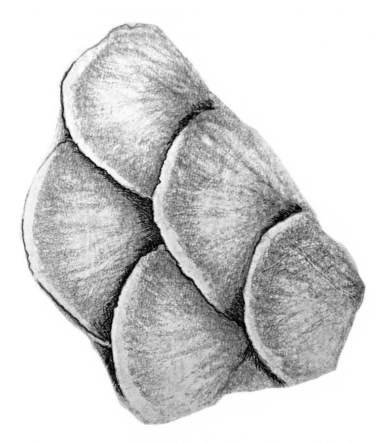

"I was so happy," the mermaid continued, "I ran to Kristian in secret and told him I would be with him the next day, and that we would be together forever. I didn't say how, but I told him I had found a way to escape. We agreed to meet the next night down by the lake. That night when the full moon appeared, I snuck down to the lake. I did as she told me. I put on the medallion and went underwater.

As soon as I did, my legs turned into this tail. My blonde hair turned white. And I could breathe underwater. But I couldn't leave the lake! Can you understand how destroyed I was? Then she was there, the medicine woman, on the lakeshore. There with him. The king. The two of them saw me in the water and laughed. The king told me I got what I deserved. If he couldn't have me, he said, no man would. Then they laughed and left me alone.

The next night Kristian came. I didn't know what to do. Would he still love me? Would he still want me? I had no idea how to break the spell. But Kristian looked and looked for me, calling out my name. I had to do something. So I worked up my courage, swam up close to him, and called out.

As soon as I did, a look of horror struck his face. He looked terrified. I called out again. This time, Kristian pulled his sword and ran away from the lake.

Aurelia shook with a loud sob. Sam held her closer. She continued, somehow even sadder than before. "I've come to realize that humans don't hear my real voice, Sam. When I try to talk to them, they hear a terrible screeching. I've tried everything. Talking softly, loudly, singing, whispering, shouting—everything. All they hear is a terrible, shrill sound. It scares them.

Just like it scared Kristian. He never returned to the lake again. I'm sure he sailed back to Norway with the rest of them after..."

Sam was tearing up, sharing in Aurelia's grief. "After what?" he asked softly.

Aurelia shook her head. "They tricked me. Cursed and placed in this wretched pool of water and left without my love. How could she do it? How could anyone do such a thing?"

"I'm so sorry," Sam said.

"But that little medallion around your neck," Aurelia said, sounding stronger now. "That medallion has indescribable power. You know, I'm not even sure the medicine woman even knew how much power it really has."

"What do you mean?" Sam asked anxiously.

"The ship? All my treasures? You asked what happened to the Vikings." Aurelia smiled mischievously, nodding over to the rotting ship. "This was King Gerald's flagship. He came with a dozen other boats. Only one returned. Kristian's ship. The one I let go."

Sam blinked at her. "What, what do you mean you let it go?"

Aurelia sat up and stared straight into Sam's eyes. "I took my revenge, Sam. On all of them. Especially the medicine woman."

Sam was speechless. Without meaning to, he started rubbing the medallion with his thumbs.

"They thought they could leave me here? They thought they could just climb onto their ships, sail down through the river to the sea like nothing happened?"

Her lips twisted into a sneer. She reached out and touched the medallion. When she did, the center stone went from glowing green to a glowing dark blue. She turned to glare back at the Viking ship. "With the medallion's help, I took my revenge."

Her last word echoed loudly around the walls of the cave. Sam felt uneasy. All this talk of curses and revenge… Aurelia seemed darker, more dangerous than before. Sam swallowed hard.

"You should take it back then," Sam said. "The medallion." A slight hint of fear tremored through his voice.

Aurelia turned back to Sam. He flinched. She tilted her head to the side, as if she recognized something. Then she smiled and took Sam's hand. He understood how sad and bitter Aurelia had gotten from her situation. She laid her head back in his lap.

Again, Sam felt calm. Serene. Entranced. Aurelia gazed up at him, her eyes now glowing with a softer green.

"No Sam," Aurelia whispered. She lifted her webbed hand up to his cheek, her long blue nails glimmering. "It is my gift to you. I will communicate with you through it. After all, that's how you found me. You deserve to keep it."

"So that's how I can hear you?" Sam asked, "With the medallion?"

"Mmmhm…" The mermaid said with her eyes bright. A few strands of silver hair laid over her cheeks.

"This little medallion is so enchanting," her voice echoed against the cave walls. "It's like it has a mind of its own. As long as you can master the medallion, you will see how much it will help you in return for helping me."

"How have I helped you?" Sam asked skeptically as he analyzed the medallion around his neck.

"By listening," she said, blinking up at him kindly. "By being my true friend."

"I'm happy to be your friend," Sam said, lost in her eyes. "Or more… I mean, whatever you need. I'll do it. I want to help you."

"Don't worry, Sam," she whispered. "You will."

Aurelia stared softly up at Sam. Her voice, her eyes, everything about her drew Sam towards her. He was overcome with the desire to kiss her again. Slowly, Sam bent down towards her. Her smile widened.

"My dear Sammy," she whispered.

Aurelia's fingers found the back of Sam's neck. His body tingled at the touch. She closed her eyes. He bent lower, their lips growing closer. Just as Sam closed his eyes and lowered for the kiss, Aurelia rolled away.

"Come on, Sam," she insisted. "Time to take you back to the surface."

"Oh!" Sam was shocked out of the moment. "Oh," he repeated, sadly, "Okay then."

Aurelia giggled. Her voice echoed like bubbles. "Don't be upset, silly. We have all the time in the world."

"Yeah," Sam said, looking down at his feet, wondering why he thought she would kiss him again. She might be three hundred years old, but in her own way, she was sixteen. Sam was only fourteen. There was no way a woman as beautiful as her would want to be with him, anyway. Never mind the age difference.

Aurelia laughed out loud. "Oh, Sam!" she said. "If you could see the look on your face."

"Oh yeah? Ha," Sam half-heartedly chuckled, kicking at the sand at his feet.

"You're forgetting something," the mermaid said in a singing voice.

"Yeah? What?"

"You need to breathe underwater." With that, the mermaid grabbed Sam and kissed him passionately. This time she held him longer and tighter. Sam responded immediately, kissing her back. Their bodies pressed into each other.

Suddenly, oxygen poured through his mouth and into his lungs again. And the kiss lingered for a moment longer.

Finally, Aurelia pulled away. Sam opened his eyes first and was amazed to see the look of happiness and tranquility in the mermaid's eyes when she finally opened them.

"Wow, Sam," she breathed.

"Wow, what?" he asked.

"Just—wow." Aurelia shyly turned away and pulled Sam into the icy water.

***

Near the shore, their heads erupting from the water broke the stillness of the lake. Aurelia watched as he waded onto the sand and turned to face her.

"Will you come and see me again, Sam?" Aurelia asked.

"Of course! I have to," Sam managed to say as he swallowed the lump in his throat. "I want to help you with whatever you need me to do."

"Thank you, Sam," Aurelia whispered. "The time is coming when you will help me. I know you will."

Sam could only stare at her fragile features and soft, pale skin. The moonlight fell on Aurelia's face and made her glow. Water drops beaded off her hair, falling gently into the lake. Her eyes twinkled inside their soft green glow.

"You can't tell anyone. About me or what I showed you. No one."

"I won't," Sam said sharply. "I promise."

Aurelia smiled sweetly. "I know."

She turned away and prepared to dive but then stopped and turned to look over her shoulder back at Sam.

"I trust you."

With a final smile, the mermaid kicked out her tail and dove under the water.

Immediately, Sam's heart sank. He missed her already.

"I trust you too," Sam whispered to himself.

A chilly draft sent shivers down his spine. Sam quickly found his clothes and put them on.

Sad to be leaving Aurelia, lost in the memory of her, Sam trudged through the forest, not even feeling the branches as they scraped against his skin on the overgrown trail.

He didn't even register the hawk's screeching cry, as Sagitta called down to him from her high pine branch, before flying away.

CHAPTER SIXTEEN

Jessica

On Monday, Sam walked down the noisy hallways of his school and finally reached his classroom. He was ready for the field trip to Mount Desert Island. He wore his favorite hiking boots and had packed his lunchbox. When Sam walked into the class, he felt like he had entered a zoo. All of his classmates were out of their seats, running around, screaming and throwing crumbled up paper balls at each other. The teacher hadn't made it into the classroom yet.

Then Jessica, the beautiful brunette, stood up at the front of the classroom and cupped her hands around her mouth. "She's coming!"

All the students ran to their seats, including Sam. The doorknob squeaked as Mrs. Hulbert entered. She closed the door behind her and turned to find the quiet students writing morning notes in their journals.

"Wow!" Mrs. Hulbert said in awe. "Just look at my perfect angels, all ready to learn." Mrs. Hulbert smiled as she set her laptop and oversized purse down on her desk.

Is she being sarcastic, Sam wondered, *or is she really that clueless?*

Even this far into the school year, Sam could not tell.

"I have a few important things to talk about with all of you," Mrs. Hulbert stated. All thirty pairs of eyes looked up at her, curious.

"As you know, we have our spring field trip today. I know that you are all excited, but I want you on your best behavior. We will leave to meet in the auditorium with the other classes in about a half hour. Also, as you know, we are reaching the last days of the school year. That means it's almost time for our annual school dance."

Sam looked up from his journal with wide eyes. Everything Mrs. Hulbert said after was unimportant. He looked across his desk at Jessica, who was writing and simultaneously twirling her finger through her long hair. The way she did it reminded him of Aurelia doing the same with her silvery hair.

It was funny. Now that he had met Aurelia—and kissed her—Jessica didn't seem so unreachable. After all, if Aurelia had enjoyed kissing Sam, wouldn't other girls?

Sam stared at Jessica, feeling more and more confident. Aurelia had enjoyed kissing him, yes, that had been obvious. Sam smiled to himself. Apparently, he was a good kisser!

Just the other day, Jessica had been the most beautiful girl he had ever seen. But now there was Aurelia. No one could beat her in the looks department. But even though Aurelia was technically three hundred years old, she was really just a sixteen-year-old girl, trapped in time.

Sam shook his head.

It hadn't registered with him but now, sitting in the classroom without the medallion around his neck, he started seeing things a bit more clearly. No matter how much Aurelia seemed to like him, she was still older than him. Sam let out a sigh.

Jessica swung her head around, flipping her hair back. Sam reddened. All year long it had been Sam's wish to go to the school dance with Jessica. Now there was Aurelia, but there wasn't really any way to take a mermaid to the school dance now, was there? Plus, her being in the lake was a big secret. He wouldn't betray her trust.

After the night he spent with Aurelia, Sam felt braver. And stronger. Like maybe Jessica *would* go to the dance with him. Why wouldn't she? If Aurelia liked him, shouldn't Jessica?

All right, he thought to himself, *it's time to be a man and finally ask her out.*

Aurelia wouldn't mind. How could she? After all her talk about Kristian, it only felt fair for Sam to at least take Jessica to the school dance.

Sam felt his confidence rise. He took his pen and pulled out a sheet of paper. On it, he wrote:

Jessica, will you go to the school dance with me?

Then he folded up the piece of paper. Mrs. Hulbert was writing on the chalkboard.

"Psssst, Jessica," Sam whispered.

She turned. Sam looked her straight in the eye and reached out with the note. Jessica raised her eyebrows, but took it. She put her pen down and slowly unfolded the piece of paper. As soon as she read what Sam had written, the bell rang. Without even looking back at Sam, Jessica packed up her backpack and grabbed her things. Sam was left without a clue of her reaction to the note.

"Who's ready for Mount Desert Island?" Mrs. Hulbert said excitedly.

The students picked up their bags and exited the classroom. Sam stood with his bag in his hand, the last one in class. Mrs. Hulbert had her purse over her shoulder and stood with the door open.

"You coming, Sam?"

Sam looked down. "Uh, yeah… just had to make sure I didn't forget anything."

You know, he thought, *like how Jessica forgot to even give me the time of day."*

Once Sam walked through the doorway, he picked up his pace to catch up with the rest of the students. Up ahead, Jessica was walking and talking with her two girlfriends, Briana and Stacy. Stacy turned to give Sam a look, then spun back to whisper something to Jessica. They all started giggling.

Giggling, Sam thought. *They're giggling. Is that a good thing or a bad thing? I have absolutely no idea.*

Briana and Stacy stopped walking, leaving Jessica alone. Sam took the opportunity to walk up.

Walking next to her for a moment, silently, he finally cleared his throat. "Jessica?" It came out as a squeak.

Jessica stopped walking and turned to Sam. She flickered her long lashes and effortlessly tossed her perfect brown hair over her shoulders.

Sam swallowed. "Well?" he said. "What do you think?"

Jessica grinned. Playfully, she waved his note in the air, then brought it close to her lips. Sam raised his eyebrows.

"Is that a yes?" Sam let out a nervous laugh.

Jessica bit her bottom lip. "Listen, we—I mean I think it's nice of you to, like, write me a note, but I'd honestly rather you ask me out in person."

"Okay, Jessica. Will you go –"

"Wait," she interrupted, placing her finger on his nose. Sam could smell strawberries and pencil lead on her fingers.

"Not like that," Jessica said. She turned to Stacy, who nodded. Then Jessica leaned in close to whisper in Sam's ear. "I want you to ask me out in front of everybody."

Before Sam could say another word, Jessica turned and joined her two girlfriends. They started whispering again as they entered the auditorium.

Ethan caught up with Sam.

"What was that all about?" Ethan asked munching on another chocolate bar he snuck in with his backpack.

Sam shook his head. "I wish I knew."

Alex pulled them into the auditorium, saying, "Come on, fellows. This field trip is sure to be educational and entertaining."

Ethan rolled his eyes.

The auditorium was already full of excited middle-schoolers. Not everyone was hoping for the enlightening experience Alex was, but any field trip was exciting. A break from the routine, a day without classes. And this trip was one of the biggest events of the year.

Sam, Ethan, and Alex found seats. Alex looked at Sam quizzically. "Why do you look so confused?" Alex asked in his Romanian accent.

Sam shrugged. "Girls are so complicated."

Ethan whistled in agreement. "Tell me about it."

"Who?" Alex asked. "Which girl is complicated?"

Sam nodded his head toward Jessica.

"Oh no," Ethan said. "Don't do it, man. I'm warnin' ya. She thinks she's all that."

"Who thinks she's all that?" Tommy, one of the class bullies, leaned forward from his seat behind them.

"None of your business, Tommy," Sam snapped.

Just as Tommy opened his mouth to say another word, Mrs. Hulbert walked past and cleared her throat loudly.

"Boys," the teacher said sternly. "Quiet, please." She walked away.

Tommy sat back in his seat. Ethan elbowed Sam, a look of shock on his face. Tommy was the toughest kid in their grade.

Sam continued, ignoring both Mrs. Hulbert's words and Ethan's silent warning, "So I asked Jessica out to the school dance. But she said I have to do it in front of everybody. You know. Probably to feel special or something."

Alex scratched his head. "Hmmm, makes sense. High maintenance girl."

"I don't know Sam," Ethan said. "I don't trust…"

Tommy's head suddenly appeared between them. "You really think you can get a date with her?" Tommy sneered. "Ha!" he leaned back into his seat, laughing.

"Boys!" Mrs. Hulbert appeared out of nowhere. "I won't tell you again. Be quiet."

At that moment, Principal Marvin walked on stage and stood at the podium. He began talking to the students about safety regulations and staying with the chaperones during the field trip.

Sam wasn't listening. His eyes were on Jessica. Then she looked back at him, along with her two girlfriends, giggling again.

"Guys," he whispered to his friends. "She keeps looking over and smiling at me."

"Yeah, you're right," Alex agreed.

"No way," Ethan whispered. "Don't trust her."

"Why not?" Alex asked. "She's obviously interested."

Ethan scowled. "All of a sudden you're an expert on girls? I'll bet you've never even held a girl's hand."

Alex brushed it off with a shake of his head. "Listen," Alex said. All three boys huddled closer. "Jessica wants attention. So give it to her. Do something special. You like her. So take a chance."

"Yeah," Sam nodded, "but like what?"

Principle Marvin ended his announcements and the entire auditorium filled with hundreds of hushed conversations. The students had a few minutes before the buses were ready to take everyone to Mount Desert Island.

"Do it now," Alex encouraged, nudging Sam's arm.

Ethan shook his head. "Don't do it, Sam."

Jessica turned from Stacy to look at Sam. Her hazel eyes gleamed. She tilted her head and raised her eyebrows as if asking him a question.

I can do this, Sam thought. *It's now or never.* He stood up.

"No!" Ethan warned.

"Yes!" Alex countered.

Sam knew what he had to do. He walked out of his seat and slowly made his way to the stage. No one seemed to notice.

"What's he doing? Ethan hissed.

"Taking a chance," Alex answered. "It's very romantic, no?"

"Romantic?" Ethan grimaced. "It's not romantic. It's suicidal."

Sam's legs seemed to move on their own. He knew what he wanted to do, but it felt like a dream. Before he knew it, Sam had walked up the steps and onto the stage. Then he found himself standing behind the podium. He looked over at Jessica, who blinked at him in surprise. Briana and Stacy whispered to each other excitedly.

Sam took a deep breath and grabbed the mic. In his most professional voice he said, "Attention everyone. Uh, I have a special announcement to make."

The room went silent. Kids nudged each other. Teachers looked at each other in confusion. Everyone stared at Sam.

Sam looked over at Ethan and Alex for last minute support. Alex gave him a thumbs-up. Ethan gave him a thumbs-down.

"Um, I would like to ask a very special girl out to a very special event." Sam looked at Jessica and pointed at her with his open arm.

"Jessica Avalon... will you go to the dance with me?"

Sam smiled brightly and waited for Jessica to say yes. He had done it. He had made her feel special. It hadn't been that hard after all.

Hundreds of heads turned from Sam to Jessica. The whole auditorium was silent. Even the teachers were staring, caught off guard.

Jessica looked shocked, but Stacy cuffed her hand and whispered something into Jessica's ear. Then she nodded, raised her head, and stared at Sam, quietly.

"Um," Sam said. "So. Will you?" This time, smiling took effort.

A smile spread across Jessica's face. Sam's heart leapt. She turned to her friends one more time. Stacy nodded, her eyes flashing. Jessica turned back to Sam and her grin turned into a scowl, like she smelled something rotten. But when she opened her mouth to answer, Stacy shouted out loud for her friend, "No way!"

Sam's mouth fell open, "but… Jessica?"

"Ha!" Tommy added. "Get off the stage you freak!" The auditorium exploded in laughter.

"Sam!" Mrs. Hulbert grabbed Sam's arm and yanked him from the podium. Caught off-guard, Sam fell into Mrs. Hulbert's arms. The two of them stumbled a few feet, catching their balance. Again, a huge wave of laughter erupted.

Things went slow motion for Sam. Mrs. Hulbert was shoving him off the stage.

Kids were laughing at him, pointing.

The cruel laughter was so loud that Sam covered his ears. Stacy was laughing so hard that tears were streaming down her face.

Sam slowly made his walk of shame back to his seat, feeling like the air was as thick as water. Finally, he reached his seat. Ethan and Alex were speechless. Sam sat down and buried his face in his palms.

Tommy thrust his face next to Sam's. "Told you she'd never date you, you loser!"

"Quiet down everyone!" Mrs. Hulbert demanded into the microphone.

"Quiet!" Mrs. Hulbert grabbed the microphone with her hand and a loud, high-pitched sound screeched through the auditorium speakers. The students covered their ears. Principal Marvin rushed over, fumbled frantically with the microphone, and finally switched it off.

But then, something eerie happened.

The feedback screech didn't go away. In fact, it grew louder and even more piercing. It sounded like an unearthly scream, like someone — or something — was dragging its sharp fingernails down a huge blackboard.

Then it started fading away... but quickly came back again, even louder. The shrill sound came back and forth, in waves. Kids started screaming, adding to the terrible explosion of noise.

"We're haunted!" one girl yelled.

"It's 'the yearning!'" a boy shouted.

"It's Sam's fault!" Tommy screamed. "He did it!"

Again, all eyes turned to Sam. He put up his hand to object and at that exact instant, the sound stopped.

Everything was dead silent.

Tommy gawked at Sam. He hadn't really meant it, that Sam had caused the screeching, but like everyone else in the auditorium right now — it certainly seemed like Sam had stopped the sound by raising his hand.

Gasps echoed throughout the auditorium. Students whispered to each other.

"All right, all right, everyone calm down," Mrs. Hulbert shouted. There was a slight hint of fear in her voice. "As many of you already know," she said loud enough to be heard without the mic, "there is ongoing research at Moon Lake and of course an explanation for these sounds…"

"Yeah, it's Sam's fault!" someone shouted from the back of the auditorium. Kids nodded in agreement and fear.

"I mean a scientific explanation," Mrs. Hulbert said loudly. "Some rare climate adjustments. We are focusing our studies next week on these types of changes."

Principal Marvin walked next to Mrs. Hulbert and flipped the microphone back on. "Mrs. Hulbert is correct. Although we don't condone Sam's behavior here today, we all know that he didn't cause that noise."

But the auditorium grumbled in disagreement. Loud whispers stood out.

"Yeah right."

"He made it stop."

"He's a freak!"

"That's enough," Principal Marvin said forcefully into the microphone. "The buses are ready now. We'll file out by class. Quietly."

Principal Marvin turned from the podium and walked offstage. Teachers began leading their students out the back doors and into the parking lot. Kids snuck looks at Sam, some confused and some angry — but most of them afraid.

Principal Marvin walked over to Sam. "You'd better come with me."

"Why?" Sam protested. "I did nothing wrong."

Ethan barged in, loudly. "Yeah. C'mon, Mr. Marvin. Give him a break," he said with a disarming chuckle.

"I mean, what if Sam really is responsible? If you say no to him, the whole school might get haunted for real. Ghosts might turn everyone into ugly creatures. Oh no, look! We're too late! It's already happening to Jessica!"

"That's enough, Ethan," Mr. Marvin scolded.

Kids around Ethan laughed. Jessica's face turned red as she gave Sam one last look before turning around. Sam had to wonder. Did she just look — sorry?

Stacy and Briana turned to give Sam one last, nasty look.

"Weirdo," Stacy hissed.

Sam bowed his head in embarrassment. Principle Marvin pushed his glasses up the bridge of his nose.

"Sorry, Sam. It's best that you do not attend the field trip today."

CHAPTER SEVENTEEN

Echoes of Moon Lake

Sitting on his bed, Sam tried to clear his mind of what had happened at school. His mom had picked him up from the office. As far as she knew, all he had done was just made a fool of himself in front of the school. So she didn't go too far in asking questions.

The eerie sound haunted Sam, bouncing back and forth inside his head. It had been the same shrill sound that he had heard at the lake, that was for sure. Aurelia had explained it. It was how her voice sounded to anyone who wasn't wearing the medallion, because of the Viking witch's curse.

Sam looked down at the medallion around his neck. He had put it on as soon as he had stepped into his room, just in case he heard Aurelia's voice again.

What was it she had been saying? Sam wondered. *And how had she made that happen at school when she must have been down at the lake?*

Sam rubbed the stone with his thumbs.

Immediately, the confusing questions troubling him were silenced. Sam felt like he was in a warm cocoon. He was calm. Safe. Strong and ready for anything.

Later, he thought. He would ask Aurelia how she had made her voice heard all the way at school. There was no rush. But first, Sam was supposed to visit Mr. Brown. Today was the day he had asked Sam to come back, so he could finish his story about Moon Lake.

Sam dialed the old man's number. They hadn't set a specific time to meet, and Sam was eager to see if he knew anything about the mermaid. But the call went straight to voicemail.

Darn it. Sam hung up and dialed again, hoping Mr. Brown simply hadn't heard his phone. But again, no answer. Sam left a message this time, asking to call him back.

As soon as he set the phone down, Sam heard the front door open. Julia's loud, high-pitched voice echoed through the house. "Leah?!"

"Geez," Sam shouted for Julia to hear, "don't you even knock?"

"I let her in," came Sam's mother's voice. "We arrived together."

Sam walked out of his room just as Julia was making her way up the stairs, which was difficult, given how she swung her hips from side to side in her tight, short skirt.

"Leah, are you ready to go to the party?" Julia's girly voice was too loud, as if wherever she went, she needed everyone to know that she was there.

Sam stood at the top of the stairs.

Julia was holding her cell phone in one hand, car keys in the other. When she reached the top of the stairs, she tossed her long blonde hair over her shoulder. Sam stared at Julia in silence. Julia stared right back at him.

"Uh. You're in my way." Julia said folding her arms over her chest, mocking Sam.

Leah called from her room. "I'll be out in just a sec!"

"Well?" Julia said, raising her eyebrows. Sam had to admit—Julia looked very grown up. And she looked good.

Julia pushed Sam aside, barged into Leah's room, and slammed the door behind her. Sam scowled and went back into his room. Through the wall, he couldn't help but hear the girls talking.

Julia was saying, "You look so cute! Josh will totally love your outfit."

"Thanks. You look amaz! Is Marcus coming?" Leah asked.

"I don't know. Probably." Sam heard the bed squeak as Julia must have sat on it. "He's super shy. I don't understand how he's so popular now. Did you hear that everybody wants him to DJ at their party?"

Sam heard the pssshht-pssshht sound of Leah spraying perfume.

"No way!" Leah said.

"Yes, way!" Both girls erupted in laughter.

Sam rolled his eyes and mimicked under his breath. "Yes, way!"

Just as Sam was wishing they would hurry and leave, his wish was granted.

He heard them stomp down the stairs talking nonstop, bid farewell to his mom, and slam the door on the way out.

Sam looked out his window to see the white car race down the street, bass pumping loudly through the neighborhood. As exits go, he had to admit... it was somewhat dramatic. A part of him hoped they'd be pulled over by their dad for speeding. As he chuckled at that idea, the house phone rang. Sam ran to his landline, hoping it was Mr. Brown. The number displayed on the phone wasn't Mr. Brown's, but it was a pretty good second place.

"Yooo, Alex," Sam said into the phone.

"Are you up for a challenge?" the voice said back.

***

Two hours later, Alex threw his controller down to the rug.

"Sam, are you cheating?"

"No!" Sam objected, still playing the game.

"Why do you keep on winning this level then?" Alex whined.

"Mad skills," Sam said proudly with his nose in the air.

An icy breeze crept like a silent thief through the bedroom window and blew all of Alex's homework over the floor.

"It's springtime. Why is it so cold out here?" Alex said as he got up and picked up the papers scattered on the floor. His dark blue curtains billowed in the strong wind like restless ocean waves. Sam shivered and pulled his cozy hoodie tighter around him.

"Hmm... that's odd," Alex said, shutting the window. "I'm sure I closed the window before you got here. Now it's open again."

"What's the big deal?" Sam said with a shrug as he turned on the TV to prepare for the next round of games. "Your mom must have opened it."

"It's no big deal," Alex said, wiping his foggy glasses with the edge of his shirt. "It's just weird."

"Ready for a rematch?"

It was at that moment when a shrill cry came from outside and suddenly pierced the air. At the same time, the lights in the room flickered as the window flung open again with full force.

"What was *that?*" Alex asked, his voice quivering. His face turned white. The ear piercing noise slowly faded into a wind howl.

"I don't know," Sam jolted up and immediately joined Alex at the window, and both boys looked outside to investigate.

Nothing.

Nothing but icy wind howling on a chilly afternoon. Alex closed the window… again.

"How did that happen?" Sam asked skeptically.

"Maybe it was just sounds from the lake," Alex suggested hopefully. "Or a warning from the Viking ghosts?" He was unsure of what happened and couldn't hide the worry on his face. Sam stayed quiet. Darkness surrounded the house as the sun slowly dipped below the horizon.

"Okay, I'm just going to finish setting up the game," Alex said, turning his attention back to the gaming system. Sam stretched out on the comfy couch trying to relax and suddenly felt the medallion in his pocket vibrate. A mysterious sound appeared, like a distant whisper.

"Come to the lake, Sam," a faint voice echoed through his mind.

"Huh?" Sam said, thinking out loud. He reached into his pocket and pulled out the medallion. Alex was still fidgeting with the game system setup.

"You say something, Sam?" he asked, not turning away from the wires behind the TV.

"Uh, nope," Sam replied.

Sam was sure that he had heard that voice before in his room. It sounded like the whisper was underwater and far away.

"I have something to give you," the voice echoed again.

A little uneasy, Sam examined the medallion more closely. *The medallion really is powerful,* he thought

Indeed, it was beautiful and magical. It glowed and shimmered brightly with its blue-green aura and felt heavy and warm in Sam's hand. Sam felt the power seep through his hands like electricity coursing through his veins. *My little treasure.* Sam grinned as he felt a strange dizziness come over him, feeling the swirling blues and greens of the beautiful jewel pulling him in.

A soft knock tore the attention away.

Sam quickly put the medallion in his pocket as Mrs. Fisher entered the room. Her jewelry jangled with each step she took. Her hair was braided with a feather on the side that was bejeweled with a deep red ruby. Still frustrated with the match, Alex stood up and turned off the TV before his mother could ask how he liked his new video game.

"Hungry, my little ones?" she asked in her thick accent. "You've been at it for hours." There was a calm tone to her voice that sounded elegant and relaxing. "I made Romanian goulash and noodles. Would you like to join us for dinner, Sam?"

Sam took a deep breath. The smell coming from downstairs was delicious. "Oh, yes!" he exclaimed. "But I'll have to call and ask my mom first."

"Understandable," said Mrs. Fisher as she pulled her cell phone from her apron pocket. Sam took the phone and dialed his number. Moments later, permission was granted and the three of them headed downstairs.

Alex parked himself next to Sam at the table, which was nicely decorated with candles. Mrs. Fisher sat on the opposite side. Sam found himself entranced by her large hoop earrings. They reminded him of a gypsy fortuneteller.

He began to think that having an exotic parent like her would be a lot of fun. A stomach rumble brought Sam out of his thoughts.

"What is Romanian goulash?" Sam inquired.

"It is a specialty from my country," replied Mrs. Fisher. "It is noodles mixed with beef, onions, and paprika."

Sam's mouth watered as he sat staring at the dishes, but neither Alex nor his mother touched the food. So Sam waited patiently.

His patience was finally rewarded when he heard the upstairs door to Alex's father's "secret office" open. Sam turned toward the stairs just in time to see Mr. Fisher sliding down the railing of the stairs naughtily.

"Sorry to keep you waiting!" Mr. Fisher said as his feet hit the ground. Alex looked embarrassed and delighted in equal measure. Sam thought that was the coolest thing he'd seen a dad do in ages. Mr. Fisher strode to the table, poured a glass of deep red wine for himself and his wife, nodded at Sam, and sat down with a contented sigh.

Marcus scuttled out of his room and darted to the table. Everyone closed their eyes as Mrs. Fisher offered thanks to the Creator in Romanian.

Sam quickly ate his plate of goulash and already asked for seconds. *Man, these meatballs are like no other!* They were so good that Sam didn't realize that he had already finished his second plate before any of the Fishers had even made it through their first.

"This goulash is wonderful, Mrs. Fisher."

"I am glad you like it," she responded, carefully sipping from her glass of wine.

A loud knock at the front door resounded through the house. As though expecting it, Mr. Fisher instantly got up from the table and answered.

Chief Larson stood on the porch. When his eyes found Sam, he seemed to frown.

"Ah, Chief Larson," Mr. Fisher said. "Please come in. Hungry?"

"No, no," the police chief said in his deep voice. "I'm still on duty. Here are this week's files. You'll see that we've received new reports. Including," he paused, again eying Sam, "the disturbance at the school."

Sam looked down at his empty plate as Chief Larson handed a manila folder to Mr. Fisher.

"I will look into them immediately," he responded calmly.

"Keep me posted. We need to get to the bottom of this. As soon as possible." With one last look at Sam, Chief Larson walked away. Mr. Fisher closed the door and sat back down at the table.

No one said a word, but Sam could feel them all looking at him.

Finally, Marcus looked up at the clock on the wall and said something in Romanian to his mother. Mrs. Fisher nodded. Alex wiped some sauce from his chin and asked, "Where are you going, Marcus?"

Marcus ran his fingers through his dark hair and said, "I've been asked to DJ for my friend's party. He lives by the lake."

Sam glanced up. Mr. Fisher was squinting at Marcus through his round wire glasses.

"Moon Lake?" Mr. Fisher asked skeptically.

Marcus cleared his throat. "Yes."

Mr. Fisher exhaled loudly. Sam shot his eyes down at his plate again, but his ears perked up and his heart started beating heavier.

"You know that Moon Lake is undergoing certain *research*," Mr. Fisher intoned. "I don't think it's best to interfere with-"

"Yes, I know father," Marcus interrupted. "I promise I won't go near the lake."

Mr. Fisher sighed. "All right then."

Marcus picked up his plate and took it to the kitchen before heading off to his bedroom.

Sam took a deep breath and finally had the courage to ask, "What's going on with the lake?"

Alex turned to Sam with a questioning look. Then his father stared at him for a moment before saying, "Moon Lake is very dangerous. Especially at night. I'm sure you know that there have been very strange noises happening recently. And, of course, at your school."

Sam gulped, but nodded in agreement. The silence hung heavily. Sam needed to change the subject. "But I had no idea you were working with the police department."

"Yes. It's classified information. I'm sure you understand how that works. But my research has proven to be very beneficial to the police department out here in Moon Lake."

Classified information? Sam thought. *How much does he really know? Does he know about Aurelia?*

Sam thought for a long moment. He would have to be careful. But he needed to know what Mr. Fisher knew.

"You don't have to worry about classified information. My dad deals with that kind of stuff all the time as the sheriff."

Mr. Fisher kept staring at Sam. Growing nervous, Sam raised his hand to his chest. Under his shirt, he felt the medallion. Warm courage flowed through his veins. Sam got an idea.

"And, you know, my dad already told me everything about the Viking legend of Moon Lake," Sam lied.

"Oh really? What do you know about the Viking legend?" Mr. Fisher asked, raising one eyebrow.

Clutching the medallion through his shirt, Sam sat up a bit straighter. "Well, for starters, I know there is a secret about Moon Lake."

Mr. Fisher nodded his head slowly. "Yes, indeed, this town has a lot of legends and secret myths. I've been researching them. And I'm very close to the solution of where the eerie sounds are coming from."

Aurelia! Sam thought. *Does he know?*

Sam gulped hard. Now Mrs. Fisher and Alex were both staring at him curiously. But he stood his ground. He wouldn't be caught in the lie. In his fingers, the medallion pulsed with power. He couldn't let Aurelia be discovered by this mad scientist.

"Actually, Sam," Mr. Fisher said calmly, "correct me if I'm wrong, but I do recall that you were lost in the forest, right next to the lake. We rescued you. It's not the only time you were out there in the forest, alone. Right?"

Darn it! How much does he know? Sam's mind whirled, wondering what to say next. Suddenly, he felt like he was playing a game of chess with Mr. Fisher. Or rather, he felt like it was a game of cat and mouse. And Sam was the mouse. The medallion pulsed hotly on his chest.

Alex turned to look at Sam. "When did that happen, Sam? You never told me you got lost at the lake."

"Hold that thought," Mr. Fisher said, standing up and leaving the table. As he climbed the stairs, Marcus came out of his room pushing a cart with loud speakers, a turntable and an large headset.

"Looks like your party will be a lot of fun," Mrs. Fisher said as she poured herself another glass of wine. But Sam could feel it. Her eyes were on him the whole time.

"This town will get a taste of Europe's best music," Marcus said as he pushed the large cart out the front door.

Mr. Fisher ambled down the stairs this time, not the railing. Sam heard every step he took on the hard wooden floors as Mr. Fisher came to stand behind him. Sam felt his heart beating faster and faster. He didn't look up, but then Mr. Fisher held out a piece of paper right in front of his eyes.

Sam forced himself not to react. He instantly noticed something unusual about it. It was a sketch drawing with some writing on the side. His breathing got heavier. The drawing. It looked very similar to the medallion, but not exact.

"Have you seen something like this before?" Mr. Fisher asked sternly, holding the paper up right.

Instinctively, Sam shook his head quickly. "Nope. I haven't seen this before."

Sam looked away from the paper. His eyes found Alex's mother. She swung her feathered braid over her shoulder and tilted her head, as if studying Sam's face. Sam focused on the feather in her hair. *Can she tell I'm lying? Maybe she really is a fortuneteller gypsy.* Sam didn't dare look into her eyes directly, as goosebumps appeared on his arms.

Then Sam felt a flush of anger. He pressed his hand against his chest, holding the medallion closer. Mrs. Fisher carefully studied Sam's eyes, as if she were looking into his soul. His face got hot with nervousness.

Why are they questioning me about my beautiful medallion? Sam thought angrily. Alex had stopped eating and watched the conversation unfold from one end of the table to the other end, like it was a tennis game.

"Um, Mom? Dad?" Alex's face betrayed his bewilderment. "What's going on?"

"Nothing, dear," Mrs. Fisher smiled. She sipped her wine and raised her eyebrows at Sam. The warmth of the medallion on Sam's chest matched the heat he felt in his heart as he started to grow more and more angry.

It's mine, he thought. *I can talk about it or not. They should just mind their own business!*

Alex's dad sat back down in his chair. He pressed his lips together in a thoughtful expression for a moment, then carefully said, "This is just a sketch drawing I've collected with my studies. I do believe this medallion has some kind of a connection to Moon Lake. The Vikings were once thought to have traveled through Maine, and specifically through this town. Amongst all my studies, this medallion has always stood out to me. It is extremely important, as it is rumored to have belonged to a Viking princess… *The Medallion of Velusipa.* In legend, it has powers, strong powers."

When Sam heard this, his blood froze.

"It's beautiful," Alex said, staring at the sketch.

"Yes," Mrs. Fisher said. "But beauty can be deceptive."

Mr. Fisher nodded. "This medallion is like no other. Many magical artifacts reflect energy. They store the powers of those who created them. But the Medallion of Velusipa is different, unique. It generates energy within itself. I believe it contains one of the most powerful stones ever found."

Sam felt goosebumps rise again on his spine. Alex stared at Sam, puzzled by his reaction, but Sam was speechless. His mind raced with thoughts about Aurelia and her medallion. He couldn't let her be found by anyone, especially Alex's dad.

"Well, that's pretty interesting," Sam said. "And kind of spooky," he added with a chuckle. "Mrs. Fisher?"

Mrs. Fisher twirled her braid. Her eyes focused hard on Sam's. "Yes, dear? What is it you would like to say?"

Sam looked her straight in the eye.

"Any chance there's dessert?"

CHAPTER EIGHTEEN

The Cold Night

Sam pedaled toward Moon Lake as fast as he could. Finally to the trail, he threw his bike down in its usual spot and ran towards the familiar overgrown path to the lake. The wind blew hard, sending chills down his spine. This night was cold. Unusually cold. Sam could see his breath as he ran.

He clutched the medallion in his hand and quickened his pace, running as fast as he could but not tiring. In fact, with the medallion in his hand, he felt like he could run forever.

Arriving at the same shoreline where he had met the mermaid for the first time, Sam stopped and stared at the center of the lake. It gleamed eerily with a white tone as the moonlight reflected on it.

Sam could hear loud bass bumping from one of the houses across the lake. It was the party Julia and Leah had gone to, Sam concluded, the same party where Marcus was playing his music.

Sam found a nice dry spot on the sand and sat down. He listened carefully to every natural sound, filtering out the loud music across the lake. He made himself aware of the sway of the forest leaves behind him and the crickets singing in the trees. The sound of teenagers yelling and laughing across the lake, as well as Marcus' music, did not blend very well with the sounds of nature.

The medallion around his neck started pulsing, softly. Sam could feel the energy of it on his chest. Never taking his eyes off the center of the lake, Sam reached up and clasped it in both hands. As soon as he did, the water began to glisten and ripple. Sam leaned forward, expectantly.

Suddenly a large movement stirred in the water toward the center of the lake. He waited with anticipating eyes, eager to see Aurelia.

He couldn't see what it was, speeding toward him underwater, but it left a churning wake behind it like a small submarine. As the zooming underwater figure approached the shore, Sam stood to greet his new friend and then, to his surprise, a huge fish jumped straight up out of the water.

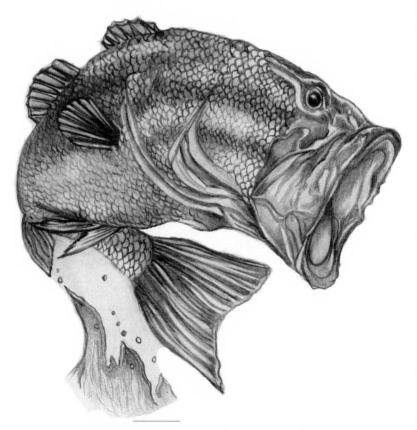

Sam couldn't believe his eyes.

There it was, just a few feet in front of him! The fish had a massive fin and huge, jagged scales. As if moving in slow motion and glistening in midair, it looked prehistoric. Its body was half the size of Sam. He stood in awe at the legendary fish that had jumped out of the water, right in front of him.

"Big Bass!" Sam shouted out loud.

The fish crashed down into the water again and was gone. The moonlight shimmered over the ripples of the water until the lake was calm again.

Sam blinked and shook his head. He said to himself, *Did that… did that really happen?*

He scanned the lake but there was no sign of the fish or any wake or ripples.

A soft, light voice spoke behind, startling him.

"Awh. He got away."

The playful voice giggled. Sam quickly turned around and saw Aurelia sitting peacefully on a rock, next to the water.

"Aurelia," Sam whispered to himself. "Thank goodness."

Her blue-green skin glowed softly. Tiny water droplets caressed her face and her mermaid tail glistened in the luminous moonlight. Water beads from Aurelia's long pale hair dripped down like a small waterfall. Sam noticed something different about the mermaid. Today she wore a headpiece made out of long seashells. It was like a crown, surrounded with smaller shells and seaweed.

Sam stood still, staring at the mermaid, once again mesmerized by her appearance. She was more beautiful than ever. A lump formed in his throat. For a moment, he forgot why he had rushed to the lake in the first place.

Aurelia smiled at him and batted her eyelashes. "Why do you look so tense, my lovely? Are you not happy to see me?"

Sam's voice squeaked. "I am happy. Very happy."

He cleared his throat and then thrust his hand out toward the lake. "But that fish! It– it's Big Bass, the one fish everyone has been dying to catch."

"Oh, that old fish?"

"Yeah, that old fish! I've been trying to catch him my whole life!"

Aurelia raised her arched eyebrows. "Really?"

She tilted her head back and let out a tinkling laugh that echoed through every corner of Sam's mind. He felt a strange warmth spreading throughout his entire body. Aurelia opened her arms, as if she could embrace the night. Then she pushed herself off the rock and dove straight into the water. A few icy drops splashed on Sam's skin and then — silence.

"Aurelia?" Sam inched to the shore to where water met sand.

Is she coming back?

And then slowly, Aurelia rose back from the surface of the water in front of Sam. Her eyes were closed. Sam sighed at her pale beauty and felt his legs tremble.

She began to hum a sweet melody. Under the water, her tail started glowing light blue. She swayed her head and hands as if casting some sort of spell.

Sam watched in silence as Aurelia inhaled a deep breath and furrowed her brow in concentration. Her humming became words.

"Great fish of the lake," she intoned slowly. "I call upon you to rise and give yourself to me."

Sam felt an unexpected rush of electricity and adrenaline pulse through his blood. Aurelia pulled herself halfway onto the sand next to Sam and turned to watch the water. Sam's eyes followed hers and he saw tiny bubbles rising to the surface of the lake just offshore. Sam's breathing quickened with excitement.

The huge prehistoric fish suddenly jumped out of the water and landed at his feet! Big Bass!

It was even bigger, stronger, and more powerful looking than Sam had ever imagined. And he seemed to be obeying Aurelia completely, lying there on the sand without struggling, as if he was just waiting for Sam to grab him.

The mermaid turned to Sam and saw how happy he was. She smiled.

"This is my gift to you," Aurelia said. "This is the oldest fish to ever live in this lake." Sam looked at her in awe. His smile squeezed his cheeks and he felt his heart grow with happiness. His entire life goal of fishing was right in front of his eyes.

"I can't believe it," Sam shouted with joy. "Whoooh!"

Aurelia laughed at his excitement. But then Sam stopped and a dark look crossed his face.

"But I don't have a bucket or net big enough to carry him home!"

Aurelia reached out and touched Sam's medallion. "With this on, you can carry him over your shoulder, light as a feather."

Sam felt happiness swarm over his whole body. He thought about being on the newspaper of Moon Lake. Everyone would know that Sam Lawrence caught the legendary Big Bass. When Aurelia saw how happy her friend was, she lifted her tail and spun around on the rock, joyfully. She looked so young and beautiful. It made Sam remember why he came.

"Aurelia," Sam said seriously, "I came to warn you. You need to be careful. There's a scientist who just moved here. He's doing research on the sounds coming from the lake. I think he knows about you living here."

Aurelia straightened herself. Her tail fluke slapped the water with fierce power. Sam backed up a step involuntarily.

"You haven't told anyone about me, have you?" Aurelia looked directly into Sam's eyes. Like she was looking into his soul.

"No," Sam protested, "I promised you I wouldn't."

Aurelia continued to stare into Sam's eyes. Finally, she simply said, "Good." She raised one hand to pull the hair away from her fragile features, her long nails sparkling in the dim light of the moon.

"Ah. What is that unbearable noise across the lake?" the mermaid asked in disgust, covering her ears. An extremely cold wind blew through the trees. It was piercing. Sam shivered.

"That's the party I mentioned. Leah and her friends are all over there." Sam shrugged. His nose began to run. He shoved his hands deep into his jacket pockets.

"Your sister is over there?" Aurelia asked, her voice like bubbles rising.

"Yeah," Sam said shivering. Letting out a breath of fog.

"Did you bring friends here with you, Sam?" the mermaid suddenly asked skeptically. Her delicate features turned dark.

"No, I came alone," Sam said, "I told you, I promised--"

Aurelia held up a finger, silencing him. "Then why are there two figures coming into the forest? I can feel their presence. Are you sure you haven't told anyone about me?"

"No, I haven't!" Sam pleaded.

The mermaid slipped off the rock and slowly sank just below the surface of the water. Her eyes glowed mysteriously at Sam as she kept her gaze on him.

Sam held his hands out. "Don't you believe me?"

But Aurelia disappeared deeper under the water. A cold gust of wind abruptly hit the lake, causing ripples on its surface to shift direction. Again Sam shivered.

He knew that he didn't bring anyone. Maybe someone was spying on him. But who could it be? Mr. Fisher?

Sam looked down at the massive fish on the sand. There it was, Big Bass. There for the taking. The biggest goal Sam had ever had. But suddenly, compared to Aurelia, the fish didn't seem so important. He sighed.

With the medallion around his neck, he lifted the massive fish without any struggle. Just as Aurelia had said, it felt light as a feather. He flipped the fish onto his shoulder and walked silently through the darkness. The thought of someone following him in the forest put him on high alert.

The large pine trees swayed in the unpleasant cold night. He jumped at every sound of movement in the bushes caused by the wind. When he looked at the moon above, he noticed that it was sheltered by thick looming clouds. It was dark and mystifying.

Walking the overgrown path, he peered from left to right, carefully scanning the dense forest, when he finally noticed some movement in the distance. Sam held his breath.

Yes, further down the path, someone was there.

Between him and his bicycle.

And heading right for him.

CHAPTER NINETEEN

Take Back What Belongs to You

Sam crouched down in a bush, breathing heavily. *Who would be out here so late at night? And why?* The medallion pulsed on his chest. Sam thought back to dinner at Alex's house. How Mr. Fisher seemed to be grilling him about the medallion. Trying to trap him. Making him admit that he had it. *Why, so he could find Aurelia? And hurt her?*

Sam reached up and clasped the medallion. It felt hot in his hand. *I won't let that happen.*

The sound of someone walking the path grew closer. Sam felt his legs tighten as if ready to spring. His fists clenched as if ready to fight. The reactions took him by surprise, like he hadn't even meant them, but then he thought, *Why not? Why not fight him? If he's trying to hurt her, I'll fight him. I'll send him right back to Romania. No one will hurt her while I'm around!*

Sam crouched even lower on the ground, ready to leap out. The medallion sent waves of energy through Sam's body. He felt stronger than ever.

He almost looked forward to fighting Mr. Fisher. Like it would give him pleasure. To punch and kick him until he was sure Mr. Fisher would never hurt Aurelia. Ever.

The sounds grew closer.

Almost to the bush. Sam tensed and rocked back on his heels. He picked up a branch the size of a baseball bat and took a good grip on it. Ready to strike. Sam took a deep breath just as he heard two voices.

"Are you sure he came here?"

"I think I saw him over by the sand. Follow me."

Sam exhaled. He knew those voices. It wasn't Mr. Fisher after all.

"Hey!" Sam shouted, standing up suddenly, revealing himself from the bush.

"AH!" Alex yelled.

Ethan dropped to the ground.

"What are you two doing here?" Sam demanded.

"S-S-Sam?" Alex was stunned. "What are you... why are you holding that?"

Sam shook his head and dropped the branch.

"Man, you scared the heck out of me!" Ethan exclaimed. "Alex forced me to come out here and find you."

"How did you know where to find me?" Sam asked Alex.

Alex shrugged. "Logic. And it seemed like maybe you needed to talk." Sam reached back into the bush and slung Big Bass over his shoulder. Ethan's mouth dropped open.

"Am I seeing things? Is that... You caught..." Ethan gulped. *"Big Bass!?"*

"But how?" Alex questioned. "Where is your fishing rod?"

Sam scratched his head and thought for a moment before he said, "I caught him with my own hands."

"You what?" Alex couldn't believe it. "How?"

Ethan rushed to touch the massive fish. "Who cares! You did it, Sam! You caught Big Bass! Wait till everyone hears!"

"How did you guys find me again?" Sam faced Alex.

Alex pushed his glasses up the bridge of his nose. "After dinner I watched you take your bike and head towards the lake. Admit it, you were acting strangely."

"Me? What about your parents?"

"Yes. Sorry about that. That was strange. But I asked Ethan to come and help me look for you. You don't understand. It's really dangerous out here. I had to make sure you weren't endangered by any Viking ghosts looking for their…"

Alex stared down at Sam's chest. Sam closed his eyes. It was too late. He had left it out, on top of his shirt.

"…looking for their medallion." Alex gulped when he finally noticed the medallion hanging around Sam's neck. Sam felt like a deer in headlights and felt a heavy lump in his throat.

"Whoa, what's that?" Ethan said as he reached out to touch it, Sam knocked his hand away.

"It was a gift... I mean. It's a medallion, but it's nothing."

"So, it's true," Alex cleared his throat loudly. "Who gave you the 'Medallion of Velusipa'? Huh."

"I'm pretty sure you already know by now," Sam said. "Something tells me that I'm not the *only one* keeping secrets around here."

Alex's face fell into a dark frown and he nodded. "Yes. So a *mermaid* gave it to you then."

"A mermaid gave you that thing?" Ethan asked, looking back and forth between his friends. There was an awkward silence between the three... especially with Alex and Sam. A strong gust of wind blew past and the boys all shivered.

Ethan chuckled. "Okay. Very cute, guys. Very cute. Let's talk about mermaids and unicorns. Maybe even the Loch Ness monster while we're at it too. I'm starting to think you guys play too many video games."

Another gust of cold wind blew even harder.

Ethan shivered. "So we found Sam. Now it's freezing cold. Let's get inside somewhere. Come on, we could even go to that party."

"I have questions first," Alex said, shaking his head.

"Well. What if I don't feel like answering them?" Sam said, taking a step toward Alex.

"Whoa, guys," Ethan said. "Take it down a notch. Mermaids, medallions, Big Bass—it's all a bit much, huh? And I have the perfect solution."

"Oh, yeah?" Sam snapped, "And what's that?"

"A warm house and hot pizza!" Ethan turned around and walked back up the trail. "Plus," he added quietly, "Briana is supposed to be there."

"Look, Ethan. I don't want to go to a party, when we've got a lot to talk about, especially since Sam has a lot to hide from his *own friends*," Alex shouted, narrowing his eyes. He kicked a dry branch from the floor, knocking it into the lake. Sam and Ethan both watched the branch slowly sink into the water. Ethan studied Sam's face for a good moment before saying, "You got something' to hide from us, Sam?"

"Look, guys. I'll just tell you when the time is right, okay?"

"Hopefully it's not too late," Alex scoffed.

Ethan nodded understandably. "I trust you, Sam. No matter what. Just know that we're here for you."

Ethan sighed and started walking back up the trail. Sam gave Alex a long hard stare, as if challenging him, then brushed past him without another word to follow up with Ethan on the trail.

***

The street was packed with cars on both sides. It looked like the whole high school was there. The older kids mingling outside stared as the three younger boys parked their bikes out front. Sam took a moment to pull the large fish off his bicycle and throw it over his shoulder. There was no way Sam would leave Big Bass out of sight.

Alex watched suspiciously. "Isn't that fish a little too heavy for you?"

Sam tucked the medallion into his shirt. "Not for me."

"Hey, come on," Ethan said, "a fire pit. Warmth."

Sam and Alex followed Ethan around the side of the house, to the back. A large group of high school students were gathered around the fire, not far from where a floating dock jutted out onto the lake. Lanterns and tiny lights decorated the trees above.

The three boys parked themselves by the fire and started warming their hands. "Ah, phase one: complete," Ethan declared. "Another minute of this and I'm off to find the pizza."

Sam looked around. Julia and Leah were sitting on a log down at the shoreline with a group of girls, all of them laughing and talking. A group of older boys approached the girls. One of them, Mike, had dark hair and held a red plastic cup in his hand. He aggressively shoved the blonde boy, Josh, into the group of girls.

"Yo Josh!" Mike laughed. "Quit chatting up the girls. I bet you don't got what it takes to jump in the lake."

"Oh, yeah?" Josh responded with a huge grin. Without another word, Josh pulled his shirt off and headed to the lake. Julia nudged Leah with her elbow and Leah blushed. Josh was a football player, very tall and muscular.

Julia took hold of Leah's arm. "Let's go watch!"

"Here," Mike said to Julia. "Hold this." He handed her his red cup and then whispered something into her ear. Julia giggled and sipped from the cup. Mike grinned and pulled off his shirt. "I'll jump too!"

Several more boys and the entire group of girls followed them to the lake. One splash after the other, the teenaged boys ran and jumped into the icy waters of Moon Lake.

"I don't think that's a good idea," Alex mumbled.

The fire pit flickered behind the group of girls, casting their long shadows onto the waters of the lake. Sam saw Alex scanning the area, as if on the lookout for danger. He felt uneasy... like someone was watching him. There, in the middle of the lake, a very-faint, glowing green point of light hovered just above the surface and caught his eye. As Sam squinted, he could make out a head floating on the water.

That's Aurelia. She's watching. I can't let them see.

"Come on, let's find the food," Sam said distracting them as he started pulling Ethan.

"No way!" Ethan gasped. "I think some of these girls are gonna go in!"

Sam scrunched up his face. He knew that the hope of seeing high school girls stripping off clothes and jumping in the lake beat out all desire of pizza for Ethan. Right on cue, Josh splashed the group of girls standing by the shoreline. "Leah, come on. Get in the water!"

Leah stepped forward, elegantly toward the water.

Ethan exhaled loudly. "Brother, I'm sorry to say it but your sister is fine. Super fine. Don't hate me."

Without moving his head, Sam looked back to Aurelia. He could tell by the way her head moved that she was watching Leah.

Leah bent down to touch the water. "Ah! No way!" Leah exclaimed. "It's freezing!"

Aurelia's head sank down into the icy water. For some reason, Sam felt relieved.

But then suddenly, with a luminous flash, the mermaid crashed her large fluke onto the surface of the water. Sam gasped, seeing her tail plain as day. But then it sank, leaving no trace of the mermaid.

"What was that?" Mike asked, suddenly treading water and staring out at the lake.

"Nothing, man. Calm down," Josh said with his deep voice.

"No, I saw a huge fin." Mike declared.

"A fin? Stop messing around," Josh said. "There was nothing--"

Another loud splash crashed in the center of the lake, throwing water high into the air.

"A bull shark!" Mike yelled. He scrambled out of the water, along with the other boys.

Ethan turned to Sam. "That's crazy. There are no sharks in the lake. That's impossible. Right?" But Ethan looked scared.

Alex was staring out into the water, biting his fingernails. The look on his face was clear; he was nervous to be anywhere near the lake.

Josh walked out of the lake, dripping wet from the cold water. His friends were silent as he peered out over the lake to see if there were any more disturbances.

"Stop trying to scare us," Julia finally said to Josh and his friends. She laughed and twirled her hair. "I didn't see anything."

"Let's go back inside the house," Julia suggested. The girls all agreed and headed for the back door. The older boys put on their oversized football jerseys and followed, mumbling about fish and sharks.

Ethan said with a sigh, "Briana is probably inside the house too."

"Why do you care about where Briana is all of a sudden?" Alex said. "You two are always making fun of one another."

Ethan rolled his eyes. "Duh? That's how I show someone I like them. A man's gotta do, what a man's gotta do."

Alex shook his head, but followed Ethan and Sam into the house.

As soon as they opened the door, music blasted their ears. A large crowd was dancing to the rhythmic beat in sync, throwing their hands up and screaming. Marcus had his equipment set up neatly against the wall.

His huge speakers and turntable took up an entire corner of the living room. Lights were flashing different colors and moving with the music. The high schoolers who weren't dancing were gathered in groups, talking loudly.

"Cheers to graduating!" someone shouted.

"Cheers!" the ocean of high schoolers yelled, raising their red cups in the air.

The three boys had never seen anything like it before. It was wild. And there were lots of kids drinking. The trio walked through the hallway, passing people who stared at the massive fish over Sam's shoulder.

"Wow! Look at the size of that fish!" Mike said.

"Is that Big Bass?" another kid asked.

Josh walked over. "What's going on?" Josh asked. "Hey. Did you really just bring a dead fish into my house?"

Sam frowned, but wasn't sure what to say.

"Hey!" Ethan answered. "You should be honored that this man is in your presence," he said, indicating Sam. "This is the greatest fisherman in the history of Moon Lake. He caught the legendary Big Bass! And his name is Sam Lawrence!"

Everyone who could hear Ethan turned to look at Sam in astonishment. The music bumped even harder as the beat dropped in the song.

"Wait a second, you're Leah Lawrence's little brother?" Josh asked.

"Yes," Sam sputtered.

"You mind if I borrow your fish?" he asked with a laugh. Josh winked to Mike, who nodded to three other friends. Before Sam even opened his mouth, Josh yanked Big Bass off his shoulder as Mike and the three other football players pinned Sam's arms behind him.

"Hey! What are you doing!?" Sam yelled. "That's *my* fish!"

Alex and Ethan tried to release the grips of the high schoolers, but were no match. Some of the other kids watched in silence as Josh carried the huge fish across the living room. Julia shrieked when she saw it. "Ew, Josh! Get that away from me!"

"Kiss it!" Mike yelled.

"Kiss it, kiss it!" other kids started chanting. Josh laughed and started inching the huge fish toward Leah's mouth.

Sam felt the medallion around his neck vibrate. Inside his head he heard Aurelia's voice, just as clearly as if she was whispering in his ear.

"Take it, Sam. Take back what belongs to you."

Warm energy flowed from the spot where the medallion hung on his chest. The feeling of strength and confidence spread throughout his entire body.

Sam was completely energized and ready to battle. He broke free and pushed the high school boys off of him. They all fell to the floor.

With blazing speed, he crossed the living room and leapt onto Josh's back. Sam landed on Josh so hard that the massive fish fell from his hands, crashed to the ground, and shook the wooden floorboards. Marcus' music was still pumping, but Sam could feel the vibrations through his feet.

All eyes were on Sam.

Leah looked up at him thankfully, but quizzically. "Sam?"

Mike and his three friends stood up. Their shock turned to embarrassment. Which immediately turned to anger. Their eyes found Sam and, as one, they marched straight toward him.

Ethan buried his head in Alex's shoulder. "Wake me when it's over."

Sam turned to face them, raised his fists, and stood his ground.

"Wait!" Leah shouted. But Mike and his friends all pulled their fists back at the same time.

It was at this moment when the unexplainable happened.

All the windows on the lake side of the house banged open as a howling gust of cold wind raged through. Curtains flapped madly. Cups fell over, even a lamp toppled to the ground. The windows were now slamming back and forth in their hinges.

Sam watched, stunned, along with everyone else.

The music stopped abruptly and the entire party instantly went dead quiet. Marcus was staring down at his equipment, trying to figure out what happened.

Then an unbearable sound rose from the lakeside. It was painfully high-pitched and even louder than Marcus' sound system. Everyone clamped their hands over their ears to try and keep out what sounded like someone dragging their long nails across a chalkboard. Impossibly, the sound grew even louder. Kids started shouting in pain and shock. Suddenly, the windows facing the lake shattered into thousands of pieces, all at once.

Then came the chaos. Screaming and shoving, the students stampeded toward the front door, everyone trying to get outside at once, as quickly as possible.

Somehow the screeching continued to get even louder.

Sam threw Big Bass over his shoulder. Alex pulled Sam and Ethan into a small hallway off the side. He pulled the door half closed as they watched the other kids elbowing and shoving each other to get out.

Sam felt the medallion vibrating on his chest. He reached under his shirt and pulled it out. It was not only glowing; it was pulsing brightly in sync with the rise and fall of the unearthly screeches.

"Cover it," Alex shouted.

Sam knew something should be done, but he couldn't stop staring at his medallion. *It's so mesmerizing. Looking at it is enough. All I need is to look at it. Nothing else...*

A strong slap brought Sam back to his senses. Alex was standing in front of him. Sam had almost forgotten where he was and what was happening.

"Cover it!" Alex yelled again.

Sam covered the medallion completely, with both his hands. Immediately the screeching stopped.

He heard a voice in his head. The familiar voice that had spoken to him earlier. Aurelia's voice.

"*Sam!*" the mermaid called out. "*I will never let anyone hurt you. Trust me...*"

Her words echoed through Sam's mind..

"What's happening?" Ethan asked frantically.

Alex was breathing heavily, shaking his head. But Sam's eyes gleamed. His mind was focused on the power of the medallion.

Although he had felt its power several times, the strength he had felt when facing the older boys had been immense. Like nothing he had ever felt before. It was like the medallion grew in strength. And then the connection to the mermaid had been — incredible. She would protect him. And he would protect her. He gazed down at his medallion. It was amazing - like Aurelia. And he loved it.

"Come on," Alex said. "They've gone. Let's go."

But Sam could only gaze upon his prized medallion, thinking about how much power he really had.

CHAPTER TWENTY

The Unthinkable

The front yard was chaos.

Some high-schoolers were racing away in their cars, others were drinking and laughing. Not wanting to be seen, Alex pulled Ethan and Sam around the side of the house to their bikes.

Sam balanced Big Bass on the attachment he usually used for his bait box. Just as he was about to pedal away, he heard a commotion over at Julia's car.

"Come on," Alex said. "Let's get out of here."

"Hold on," Sam said.

He focused his hearing, but couldn't make out what Leah was saying to Julia. They seemed to be fighting, surrounded by some boys. Sam looked down at his medallion. He placed one hand on it. Sure enough, his hearing improved. He turned to watch the scene at Julia's car.

"Come on Julia, let's just go," Leah was saying.

"Why would we leave right now?" Julia said, laughing. She had her arm wrapped around Mike's waist.

"Stay," Mike said, pulling Julia closer and grinning. "The party just started!"

Leah threw her hands in the air. "Are you kidding? If you want to stay, Julia, that's fine. I'll find another way home."

Leah looked down and saw a half empty plastic cup in Julia's hand.

"And you're drinking." Leah said. "You've never done that before."

Julia scowled at Leah and gave her an offended look.

"Relax, *Mom*," Julia taunted.

Leah was staring daggers at her.

"Oh come on," Julia slurred, "I'm fine."

"We need to talk," Leah said, and sat in Julia's passenger seat for privacy. Julia rolled her eyes at Mike but got into the driver's seat. Mike gave Josh a high-five.

Even though they were in the car, Sam could hear them clearly.

Julia was whispering harshly. "Why do you keep controlling what we always do, Leah? I'm so over it."

"I just care about you," Leah shot back. "Look, you're not being you. You're trying too hard. Trying to show off to Mike and his friends." Leah ran her fingers through her hair and exhaled loudly.

"I'm fine!" Julia defended. She waved her hands in the air and accidentally hit Leah.

"Don't hit me. What's wrong with you?" Leah said narrowing her eyes. "You're acting weird."

"I hope you're happy," Julia snapped. "I can't believe you're going to ruin our night." Julia placed her key in the ignition and turned on her car.

Intuitively, Sam felt like he had to interfere. He jumped off his bike and started pacing toward the car.

"Look, don't worry. Stay here and hang out with Mike. I'm just going to walk home," Sam heard his sister say.

"No," Julia replied harshly, "We're leaving because you always have to be right. Ugh, you're such a…"

Sam felt a strong and horrible feeling deep in his stomach. He was now running toward Julia's car. His friends followed, catching on to what was happening.

"Unlock the car, Julia!" Leah shouted, "Please."

But Julia pushed the gas pedal down full force and whizzed right past the three younger boys, speeding down the street.

Sam's heart dropped and his breathing turned heavy. *God. Please help my sister get home safely.*

"That Julia girl's been drinking," Alex said, concerned.

"Come on!" Ethan barked.

The three of them ran back to their bikes and pedaled after the car.

A frigid breeze swept through the street as Sam's mind overflowed with concern for Leah. They couldn't see Julia's car, but knew they were following the right route. There was only one main street to take between the lake and Sam's house.

Let them be okay. Let them be okay. Let them be--

The ear-piercing sound of squealing breaks sliced through the night air, followed by a massive bang.

"No!" Sam shouted.

The three boys put their heads down and pedaled as fast as they could. With the strength of the medallion pulsing though him, Sam quickly pulled away from the other two.

Sam turned a corner at break-neck speed to see a cloud of smoke rising up into the air. He stopped his bike.

In shock, Sam's thoughts moved so slowly that at first he couldn't comprehend what had happened. He stared with panic in his eyes. Julia's car was upside down. Another car, a minivan, was stopped sideways in the street with a deep dent in its hood. Its engine was pouring thick, white smoke.

"Leah!" Sam screamed. Tears began to flow down his face. He dropped his bike to the street and raced toward the flipped white car.

The driver of the minivan, an elderly woman, yelled from her seat. "I called an ambulance!" She was struggling with her seatbelt, but didn't seem to be seriously injured.

Sam reached the white car just as Julia pulled herself out. She had cuts on her face and hands. Julia crawled a few feet from the car and sat cross-legged in the middle of the road, in shock, staring into space.

Sam watched Julia like it was all in slow motion. He was terrified to find out something serious had happened to Leah.

In the distance, Sam could hear the sound of sirens approaching. They sounded underwater, like it was all a dream. A pained cry coming from the car shook him out of it.

"Leah!" Sam yelled again. He made his way to Leah's door. It was caved in and seemed to have taken the worst of the impact.

Sam nearly screamed when he saw Leah hanging, upside down, from her seatbelt. She was limp, like a doll, but crying loudly. Blood was running down her face from a cut on her head.

"Leah! Leah, I'm here!" Sam pleaded. Leah slowly reached out her hand and Sam took it.

"Leah, hold on! The ambulance is coming," Sam cried.

"I told her to stop the car and let me out." Leah sobbed. "The door wouldn't unlock. I tried so hard."

"It's okay," Sam said, trying to be brave. "The ambulance is almost here."

Uncontrollable tears poured down Leah's face.

"Help me with my... Oh no!"

"What is it?" Sam's voice cracked with pain. His body shook in terror. It was like a nightmare that wouldn't end.

"My legs!" Leah shrieked, "I can't feel my legs!"

CHAPTER TWENTY-ONE

Anticipation

How he had gotten to the hospital waiting room had been a blur. He remembered the swirling lights of the ambulance. The paramedics. His friends waiting with him until his parents arrived at the crash scene, just as the ambulance sped away. He remembered a couple snapshots of his mother crying in the car on the way to the hospital, but that was it. They had heard no word yet about Leah's condition. Even though Mr. Lawrence was the sheriff, the doctors wouldn't let him past the waiting room.

I can't feel my legs!

Leah's words rung like a bell in his mind. He remembered the blood on her face and the way she had hung, lifelessly, from her seatbelt when he had first arrived.

God, please let her be all right. Please let her be all right…

"Mr. and Mrs. Lawrence?" An elderly woman's words brought Sam out of his painful thoughts. She was fair skinned and beautiful with a kind and elegant smile. Her eyes were an angelic blue.

Sam and his parents all rose to their feet, expectantly.

"Please come with me," the woman said with her gentle smile. Sam immediately felt her warmth.

He didn't understand how, but it was as if this woman understood everything his family was going through.

The elderly woman nodded as she gestured them to follow her. Wordlessly, the family walked through the white hallways of the silent hospital. Sam glanced around, skeptical of the quiet atmosphere. This hospital was too perfect. It almost seemed eerie. Sam's mother anxiously walked close to the older woman in the white hospital outfit but, like Sam, seemed too afraid to ask the questions burning in her mind.

As they reached the last room in the hallway, the woman opened the door and waited for them to walk through. Sam and his parents all saw Leah at the same time. She was propped up in the hospital bed. They bandaged her head, her legs were inside wrappings, her face was spotted with purple bruises—but she was alive. Leah smiled weakly at her family.

"Honey!" Mrs. Lawrence exclaimed. She and her husband both rushed to the bedside. Sam paused before he walked through the door.

The older woman whispered softly, "Go on. Your sister needs you, Sam."

Sam took a deep breath. He stepped into the room, but then stopped. "Wait," he said, turning back toward the older woman, "how do you know my name?"

But she was gone.

Sam blinked at the spot where she had stood just a moment before.

"Mom," Leah croaked behind him.

Sam's heart dropped as he turned back into the room. His mother had seated herself on the corner of the bed, while his father was kneeling down at Leah's side. Sam walked slowly to the foot of the bed. Closer now, he could see the deep, dark circles under her eyes. Most of her brown hair was pulled back into a messy knot, away from her face. The bruises were not only purple and raw looking, they were swollen. Her left eye was half closed. She had more bandages around her arms and shoulder. Tubes laced over her chest.

A lump caught in Sam's throat. She looked so fragile and weak.

"Mom, Dad… Sam," Leah managed to say. "It's so nice to see you."

Silently, Sam started to cry. *Her legs,* Sam thought. *What about her legs?* But Leah was alive. That's what mattered most.

"It's okay sweetie," Mrs. Lawrence said through her sobs, trying to sound brave. "We are here, all of us. We are here for you."

Mr. Lawrence burst into tears. Sam had never seen his father cry in his entire life. For a moment, all Sam could hear was his father's soft sobs. In the background, a medical machine beeped rhythmically.

"My beautiful girl," Mr. Lawrence murmured. "How could this happen?"

"It… it …" Leah's voice was raspy and faint.

"It happened so fast, Daddy. I told Julia to stop the car. She didn't listen to me."

Mr. Lawrence moaned and shook his head angrily. Leah's eyes floated toward Sam.

"Hey, munchkin," she whispered. "I'm..." Leah's voice faded into an exhausted sigh.

Sam took a few steps and reached out for her hand. Her skin was ice.

"What is it, Leah?" Sam breathed. His hand wrapped tighter around her cold fingers.

"I'm so glad you were the first one there," she finally managed to say.

Fresh tears streamed down Sam's face. "Leah! I'm so happy you're... alive."

None of the family noticed the white figure enter the room. The doctor cleared his throat. "I'm very sorry, Mr. and Mrs. Lawrence. But it is getting late and our visiting hours are over. We must leave Leah here overnight. She needs to rest."

"But her legs!" Sam blurted. "What about her legs?"

The doctor looked at Sam quizzically for a moment, then nodded. "Of course. You were first on the scene, weren't you? Yes, Leah lost feeling in her legs. She suffered some very nasty bruises to her back and her spine got knocked around pretty good. But her legs are fine. Sprains only. Nothing broken anywhere, no internal damage. I know she looks banged up, but she's a very lucky girl. She should make a full recovery."

Sam exhaled so loudly it came out like a gasp. He dropped his head onto Leah's thigh.

"Hey," Leah winced. "That doesn't mean you can give me more bruises, munchkin."

Somehow Sam laughed and cried at the same time.

"Thank God," Sam's father said. His mother jumped up and hugged the doctor.

"Thank you, thank you," Mrs. Lawrence was saying. Everyone knew she was talking both to the doctor and to God.

Sam's mother turned back to Leah. "We'll be here first thing in the morning, as soon as they let us. Sleep well, my baby. We love you."

"Bye," Leah whispered. Just before her eyes closed heavily, Leah added slowly, "I love you too."

Suddenly, a strong breeze blew through the open window. The drapes billowed wildly with the brisk, cold air. The doctor immediately closed the window.

"My apologies. We never keep the windows open. Not sure how that happened."

"Yeah," Leah sighed. Everyone turned to her. They thought she had fallen asleep. Groggily she said, "Who was that girl, anyway?"

"Girl?" the doctor said, cocking his head. "What girl?"

Leah nodded slowly toward the window.

"The pretty one... looking at me. The one with the..." Leah was drifting back to sleep. "With the blueish hair. It was like I could... see right through her..."

Leah closed her eyes again, peacefully.

Mr. Lawrence turned to the doctor, who nodded kindly. "It's the medicine," he whispered. "We've had to medicate her significantly for the pain."

The doctor led the family out into the empty hallway and left them in the waiting room.

Blue hair, Sam thought. *Could it be... was it...*

"Come on, Sam," his father said. "Let's get some sleep."

As Mr. Lawrence led him toward the door, he put his arm around his son's shoulders. "I need to tell you how proud I am of you, Sam. Everyone says how brave you were at the accident scene."

Lost in thought, he only nodded. His father put his other arm around his wife.

As they were walking out the door, Sam turned to look for the kind, mysterious woman who had guided them to Leah's room.

But she was nowhere to be seen.

CHAPTER TWENTY-TWO

The Plan

The sun was shining brightly in the clear blue sky. The birds outside were singing in the beautiful sunlight. Lying in his bed, Sam's thoughts were not as bright. It was Saturday and Sam would normally jump out of bed to go play with Ethan and Alex, or head down to the lake. This morning though, with Leah lying in a hospital bed, all Sam wanted to do was hide from the world in case somehow more terrible news was on the way.

He could hear his mother downstairs busily preparing breakfast. Today would be just as hard for them, he realized. Maybe even harder. With a sigh, Sam swung his legs off the bed and stood. If possible, he would be a source of strength for his parents today.

When Sam arrived in the kitchen, he noticed his mother dressed elegantly in a long blue dress. Her long, light brown hair was pulled back into a ponytail. She held a large bunch of red, white and pink roses she had just cut from her garden. But her eyes were red from crying. Sam tried not to stare at the empty chair Leah usually sat in.

"Would you like some juice, Sam?" his mother asked faintly as she placed her roses in a vase.

"Yes, thank you," Sam said politely. "I would love some."

Mr. Lawrence sat in silence staring at the paper, not looking up as Sam sat down. Sam could feel sadness and frustration consuming his father.

"Good morning, Dad." Sam tried to smile before he finally noticed the headline on his father's newspaper: *Teenage Girls Involved in Devastating Crash.*

Mr. Lawrence still didn't speak. His face was pale. He was more focused on reading the newspaper in his hand.

Mrs. Lawrence answered for her husband, "Good morning, baby. We all aren't feeling well today."

"Good... morning. Sam," his father finally muttered word by word.

"Sam," his mother's voice started to quiver. She put one arm around him.

"The doctor called early this morning. Leah has taken a turn for the worse. It seems there is internal bleeding after all." She took a deep breath, in her other hand the spatula was trembling as she stared into the scrambled eggs cooking in the pan. Sam's mom reached out for the table and then sat down and turned her wet eyes to her son.

"They... they can't explain it. They're going to run some tests but Leah will be staying in the hospital for a while. They say her condition is... critical. That's all we know for now."

No, Sam thought. *No, she was supposed to be all right!*

Sam swallowed the lump in his throat, again trying to be strong for his parents. "There has to be something we can do," Sam said.

His father looked at him, sorrowfully. "There's nothing we can do. That's the worst part, son. It's out of our hands."

"It's in God's hands," his mother said softly.

Mr. Lawrence suddenly smashed his fist on the table. "Why did this have to happen to us?" Mr. Lawrence shouted. "I could have gotten there faster. The noise disturbance came in and I dragged my feet, expecting another false alarm. I knew Leah was there with her friends. I should have acted faster."

"No one asked for this to happen!" Mrs. Lawrence exclaimed just as loudly. She placed her hands on her hips. "Don't blame this on anyone. Not even yourself."

Sam's thoughts raced to find a way to cheer up his parents. He thought about asking to borrow his father's deep-sea fishing pole, just to achieve some sense of normalcy on this weekend morning.

Wait. Big Bass! Sam suddenly remembered. For a moment, Sam wanted to cheer up his father with the mention of catching Big Bass. He opened his mouth ready to announce his fish, but then closed it as he saw a tear slip down his father's face. Sam felt worthless. His sister was in the hospital and here Sam was about to brag about the fish that was now rotting in the garage. The fish that he didn't even catch.

Sam was shocked at how loud and emotional his parents were. Seeing his parents so sad sent a knife through Sam's heart. And Leah was suddenly in danger. He fought back the tears and breathed deeply.

They need my strength. Leah needs strength. If I could just...

An idea came to him and he jumped to his feet, shocking his parents.

"I know it's difficult, Sam," his mother said, wiping her eyes. "We all feel helpless. And the waiting is the worst. We're going to let her rest this morning and go visit a bit later if you'd like to come."

Sam nodded, though his thoughts were elsewhere. He knew what he needed to do, who he needed to talk to.

"It's a beautiful day," his mother continued. "Why don't you try and have a nice morning? Maybe you can play outside with Ethan or Alex and then join us later to visit Leah."

Sam nodded vigorously. "Yeah, I think you're right, Mom." Sam crossed the room and opened the garage door. Before leaving the kitchen, he turned to look back at his father one last time.

"Don't give up hope, Pop. We're going to do everything we can for her."

Sam's father cocked his head, a question on his lips. But before Mr. Lawrence could speak, Sam said, "I'll be back in a few hours. Don't leave without me."

Rushing into the garage, Sam closed the kitchen door behind him. He leaned up against it for a moment and wiped the fresh tears off his face, the ones he had been holding back.

"Wait," his mother called through the door. "Your breakfast."

But Sam didn't answer.

Right next to his bike, Big Bass was lying, lifeless, on the concrete floor. His mouth was open and his scales were beginning to flake off. Sam realized now, in the morning light streaming through the garage windows, how majestic the fish really was. He felt a sting of guilt. Big Bass deserved to be living freely and happily in the waters of Moon Lake. He was part of history, a legend, and now the glorious creature was lying in Sam's garage, dead — for no good reason.

He shook his head at how selfish he had been when Aurelia had given him the fish.

The thought shook him from his reverie. Big Bass' death was a tragedy and Sam regretted it. But he had infinitely more important plans this morning. And he didn't have a moment to waste.

***

The wind stung Sam's wet cheeks as he raced down the familiar roads of the neighborhood. As he passed Mr. Brown's house, something caught his eye. Sagitta, the hawk, was perched on the brick chimney. When Sam looked over at the bird, Sagitta gave a screech and took off into the air.

Mr. Brown, Sam thought. *I still haven't heard from him.*

It was one more thing to figure out—after he spoke with Aurelia.

When Sam reached the park, he dropped his bike on the overgrown grass and started running down the path. An explosion of grasshoppers jumped out of his way. Sam rushed through the tall trees and bushes until he reached the secluded shoreline where he had last spoke with Aurelia.

He stood, panting, on the sand. The lake was quiet. On the other side, where the park was, there were kids swimming and jumping into the waters of Moon Lake.

"Aurelia," Sam whispered.

"Aurelia!" he repeated louder.

And then Sam remembered. *It's daytime.*

He hit the palm of his hand against his forehead, jammed his eyes shut and said out loud, "Ugh I should've known. She only comes out at night!"

"Does she?" The tinkling voice held lightness and laughter.

Sam opened his eyes and Aurelia's beautiful face gazed back at him. Only her head was above water.

"Why do you look so sad, Sammy?" the mermaid asked, pouting her lips. Sam could see her features so clearly. She was mesmerizing. Without meaning to, he smiled. He felt butterflies in his stomach again. All his troubles—and they were many—were somehow forgotten.

A gust of wind blew across his face, sending a chill down his spine. Sam's thoughts came back to him.

"Aurelia, last night... my sister got into a car accident!" Sam burst into tears. Embarrassed, he hid his face from the mermaid with his hands.

Aurelia pulled herself halfway out of the water, sat next to Sam on the shoreline, and took his hand. "Oh, my Sam. Don't cry." Her eyes gleamed with concern.

"Last night they said she'd be okay but... somehow things got worse. Much worse."

"Yes," Aurelia said, stroking his cheek. "I know."

Sam turned to look into her eyes. "You were there. Right? Leah saw you in the window."

The mermaid smiled. Sam could feel her power and beauty as if they were something he could reach out and hold in his hands.

"I was there. She's very pretty, Sam."

"I didn't know you could do that. Leave the lake. And I didn't know you could come out during the daylight," Sam said, his eyebrows furrowing.

Aurelia giggled. "My body didn't go there, silly, only my spirit." She shook her long, beautiful tail. "And I can't usually even do that. But this is the time of the hundred-year anniversary of my curse. The full moon—it's a very special time for me. Very rare. And powerful."

Then Aurelia grew serious. "I know why you came. And you're right. I do have a way to help your sister."

Aurelia looked down and touched the sand. It turned a tint of blue at the touch of her nails. The mermaid smiled at it as if enjoying the unusual intensity of her own power. Then she moved her hand over Sam's face, gently brushing her long blue fingernails over his skin. Sam couldn't see it, but his face also, for a moment, glowed with a soft blue tint. Sam felt goose bumps sprout up all over his body.

"Actually," she continued, "I have a way to help *you* help your sister."

"You do?" Sam gulped. The wind picked up in a distance.

"Yes. And the answer is already within your reach."

Sam's eyes opened wider. "What do you mean?"

"Reach into your pocket, my beloved Sam." Aurelia tossed her long, pale hair over her shoulder.

"My pocket? There's nothing in my..." And then Sam felt it.

Slowly, he pulled it from his pocket. "The medallion?"

He rubbed the gem with his thumb and it glowed mysteriously with its rich blue, purple and green colors. Aurelia smiled as she studied Sam's face for a long moment. Sam couldn't help but stare into her dancing eyes.

Finally he said, "Are you saying the medallion can heal Leah?"

A sparkle flashed in Aurelia's green-blue eyes. "Yes!"

Then she added in a softer tone, "You know how powerful it is. It has given you strength. Courage. Abilities. But it also has the power to heal."

Sam rubbed the gem harder with his thumb. The shining light grew, bathing his face in blueish tones. A confident smile spread across his face.

"Take it to her, my love. Place it around your sister's neck. Trust in me and you will see her completely healed in seven days."

Aurelia slipped back into the lake. She submerged herself completely, then rose her head up again. Beads of water glided down her hair like liquid silver. Her eyes closed and her body grew rigid as if she was summoning all of her powers.

"Give me the medallion, Sam, so that I may enchant it with my power." The mermaid reached out her hand to Sam.

Without question, Sam handed the medallion to the mermaid. She cupped her hands over it and breathed deeply, turning her head to the sky. Sam heard her chanting in a strange language.

Her skin started glowing a deep green. The surrounding water started bubbling, softly at first but quickly more and more violently.

Aurelia's chanting grew louder and louder.

Fish started jumping madly up into the air, twisting, and splashing back into the water. Sam heard a squadron of birds behind him cry out and take flight. The sky was suddenly filled with every bird squawking crazily and rushing away.

Aurelia stopped chanting.

The birds were gone.

The fish stopped jumping.

The waters stopped roiling.

An eerie silence fell.

The mermaid pulled the medallion close to her lips and whispered something into the gemstone.

Then she opened her eyes and handed the medallion back to Sam.

He could see her arm trembling.

"Sam," Aurelia whispered.

He had never seen her look tired like this.

"Hurry," she urged. "You don't have much time!"

CHAPTER TWENTY-THREE

Leah's Gift

Sam rushed into the hospital already out of breath. It had been a long, hard ride from the lake. After signing the visitor's log, Sam felt a pang of guilt in not going home first and accompanying his parents to the hospital. He had promised to go with them, but he couldn't have them around, given what he had to do and he didn't have much time.

The hospital had moved Leah to an Intensive Care Unit since the previous night. Sam was shocked at what he saw. While Leah seemed to be sleeping peacefully, the serenity of that slumber could not mask her horrifying appearance. There were frighteningly dark circles under her eyes and purplish blotches spreading out from beneath the bandages that covered much of her body.

Leah looked much worse than she had the night before. She was almost lifeless. She looked painfully thin and fragile. But it was Leah's expressive face that scared Sam the most. He had never seen his sister look so utterly... *vulnerable.*

How could this have happened overnight? When they had said there would be no permanent damage?

He intended to let Leah sleep and slip the medallion around her neck secretly, but Leah began to stir, as if sensing Sam's presence. She opened her eyes.

"Hi munchkin." It came out like a croak. Leah tried to smile, but it sent a small wave of pain through her body, making her wince. "It's so good to see you. Where's Mom and Dad?"

"They're, uh, coming later," Sam replied in nearly a whisper. "I needed to see you. Alone."

Leah cocked her head and then, Sam could tell, another surge of pain hit her. She took such a harsh breath that it made a whistling sound. Sam found himself fighting back tears for what felt like the millionth time in only half a day.

"Stay still, Leah. I brought you a present." From his pocket, Sam produced the exotic green-blue medallion.

Leah's eyes lit up.

"Do you like it?" Sam asked.

"Are you kidding? I *love* it," she whispered. "It's so beautiful."

Leah reached for the medallion, but her arm didn't have the strength. She dropped it back to the bed with a pained sigh. Sam leaned in, unlocked the necklace's ancient clasp and reconnected it around Leah's neck.

As he laid the medallion on her chest, a small jolt washed over Leah's body.

"Oh," Leah said in surprise.

"What is it?" Sam asked, watching her closely.

"It gave me a little shock," Leah said, louder than before. "Whoa," she said, "does this thing have batteries or something?"

"Why do you ask?" Sam said with a tone of hopefulness.

Leah was silent for a moment. She started blinking and shaking her head back and forth slowly. Sam's heart leapt as he noticed the color returning to her face. Leah's eyes began to sparkle.

It's working! Sam yelled to himself inside. *And so quickly!*

Leah sat up in bed. She seemed refreshed, re-energized — restored in spirit to the sister he knew, even if her body remained bloodied and battered.

"Sam," Leah said in awe. "I, I can't believe how much better I feel all of a sudden." Leah picked the medallion up in her hand and gazed at it. Sam saw a look of peace spread across her face. Her eyes unfocused. Her whole body seemed to relax.

"For the first time since I've been in here," she whispered to the medallion, "I'm not in pain. I feel... happy!"

Sam couldn't speak around the lump in his throat.

Thank you Aurelia! Thank you!

In his head, Sam heard, as clear as day, the mermaid reply. *Of course, my Sam. That is what best friends are for. They help each other.*

Sam had been too afraid of hurting Leah to touch her. But now he threw his arms around her neck and dropped his head to her shoulder. Leah returned the hug and squeezed him tight.

"Where did you get this?"

Sam pulled back, his eyes glistening. "I got it from my new friend. My best friend."

Leah grinned. "I'm not sure Ethan and Alex are going to like hearing about this new best friend."

They sat together quietly for a moment, their smiles doing all the talking. When Leah again held up the medallion to admire it, she was so enthralled by the ornament that she failed to notice the huge red hawk landing in a tree next to the window, a large fish clutched in her talons. Sam watched in awe.

Sagitta, Sam thought, stunned. *Mr. Brown's hawk.*

The hawk ruffled her feathers and then savagely devoured the fish practically whole. It was as if Sagitta had something to prove. Then, after making her statement, the majestic creature took off, disappearing into the clouds.

Sam turned to see Leah still gazing at the medallion. His heart was overflowing with gratitude, seeing her already looking so much healthier.

"Mom and Dad will be here soon," Sam said. "But can I ask you a favor?"

"Of course, munchkin," she replied, not taking her eyes from the medallion.

"Can we keep this present a secret?"

Leah nodded quickly. "Oh yes," Leah blurted, tucking the medallion under her hospital gown. "I'd rather not have anyone see it anyway. It's like... it was made just for me..." Leah's voice trailed off. Through her gown, she grasped the medallion with her fingers. Then her eyes started drooping.

"It's like," she said as sleep overtook her, "it's such an interesting feeling..."

Leah fell asleep.

Sam crept out of the ICU and headed down the hallway. Instinctively, Sam reached for the medallion in his pocket—but of course his medallion was not there. He felt a moment of loss. And then even a little bit of jealousy. He didn't like not having the medallion. Now it was he who felt vulnerable. Less powerful. Incomplete. A dark thought entered his mind.

I should have told her it was temporary. That once she was healed, she should give it back.

But he immediately felt bad for such a thought. Leah was his sister. She needed the medallion's powers much more than he did. And there was still Aurelia. He still had his new best friend. Or even something more?

Sam recalled, warmly, how Aurelia had started calling him things like "My love," and "My darling Sam." He smiled. He would head back to the lake on his bike and thank the mermaid.

As he passed a door that was ajar near the end of the hallway, Sam heard voices inside. Arguing. He recognized them both.

Sam peeked through the crack of the door, not wanting to be seen.

Yes, the two people were arguing but in hushed tones, like they were keeping their conversation a secret.

"I thought we had an understanding," the man was saying. "A trust."

"We do," a woman replied. "You know we do. Born of generations, centuries of mutual respect and benefit between our peoples."

"And yet you never thought to warn me?" the man asked.

"You must understand I am under certain restraints when it comes to my family's powers and traditions. Haven't your people kept your own secrets?"

"It appears neither of us have secrets from a certain young warrior who is eavesdropping from beyond the door. Come in, Sam."

Sam gulped. He pushed open the door and stepped inside. For the second time in less than a day, Sam was unpleasantly shocked by seeing someone he cared about in terrible condition. Mr. Brown was in bed with tubes leading from his arms and chest into various hospital machines. The lines on his face were etched deeper than Sam remembered. He looked thin and sick. Very sick.

Then the fair-skinned, angelic nurse flashed Sam a harsh look very different from the tender, heart-warming ones she had given him the night before. But then her face softened.

"Ah yes," the nurse said, "the young warrior you spoke of. This one we must be sure to keep an eye on. When he's not keeping an eye on us."

She passed Sam on the way out of the room and gave him a small squeeze on the shoulder.

"Mr. Brown," Sam said slowly. "What happened to you?"

"Young warrior," he said with a soft smile. "I knew you would find me, eventually."

"I didn't even know you were in the hospital. What... how..."

The elderly Native American man's face was the very picture of kindness. "My boy," he said haltingly, "do not be afraid. A wise man once said, 'The oldest and strongest emotion of mankind is fear, and the oldest and strongest fear is fear of the unknown.'"

He motioned for Sam to join him. Sam obliged, sitting on the side of the bed. He loved this man, Sam realized. They had not spent much time together, but the bond between them was strong. Sam even regarded him as a grandfather.

The old man sensed Sam's sudden discomfort and placed a hand on his shoulder, which made the boy feel warm and protected.

Yet, moments later, Mr. Brown became inscrutable again as he gazed up at the ceiling, as if studying the stars. As he stared upwards, Sam studied the gruesome scar running across Mr. Brown's cheek and neck.

"Remember when I told you my days on this Earth were numbered?" Mr. Brown asked. Sam nodded, anticipating another bombshell.

"It seems my departure may come even sooner than I have expected."

The news hit Sam hard. He closed his eyes, afraid to hear any more.

"Life," Mr. Brown offered, a disturbing finality in his voice, "is very short. Even when you've lived it for over one hundred and twenty years."

Sam didn't know what Mr. Brown was getting at. He certainly wasn't one hundred and twenty years old.

Was he?

Mr. Brown took a deep breath before he said, "Tell me, young warrior, what has your journey taught you? What have you discovered from the lake?"

Sam felt the need to open up to Mr. Brown completely. But he had given Aurelia his word that he would never mention her to anyone. The conflict inside him was hard to bear.

"I think the stories you told me are true," Sam finally said.

Mr. Brown nodded and looked at Sam with understanding eyes when he said, "For several generations I have been the only person alive who knows the truth about the secret of Moon Lake. And I cannot let that knowledge die with me. I'm glad that our destinies have crossed paths."

"But don't you have children?" Sam asked.

"I do. And grandchildren. And great-grandchildren." The deep wrinkles around Mr. Brown's mouth turned into a creased smile. "But as I have told you, young warrior, you are very special. More special than you even know."

The conversation was making Sam uneasy. "I need to know the rest of the story," Sam said eagerly. "What happened to the princess?"

The old man's eyes focused hard on Sam's.

"Yes, young warrior," he said in a serious tone. "You are very special, indeed. Now sit down. I may only have the strength to tell this story one time. You must listen to me more carefully than you have ever listened to anyone in your life. It will be a matter of life and death. Yours, and others. Listen to me..."

CHAPTER TWENTY-FOUR

The Warning

Mr. Brown took a deep breath and closed his eyes before he said, "Sam, where did we leave the story? What is the last thing I told you?"

Sam was grateful Mr. Brown's eyes were closed. But he also felt like this was a test of some kind. He had promised Aurelia not to speak of her with anyone. It was difficult, because of how much he cared for Mr. Brown, but Sam needed to keep that promise. His word was his word.

He thought before answering. Aurelia had told him about how she had been tricked by the Viking medicine woman and King Gerald into becoming a mermaid. She had told Sam about taking her revenge on his men and his ships — all except Kristian's ship, which she had permitted to escape. But Mr. Brown's story, back at his house, had ended much earlier in the tale.

"You told me that King Gerald took Aurelia, with him to the new world and that he had devised a plan to have the man she was in love with, Kristian, killed. And that was where you stopped."

Mr. Brown opened his eyes and gazed at Sam, silently. Then he nodded, giving Sam a chance to continue.

"Would you, uh, like some water?" Sam asked feebly, turning away. Mr. Brown shook his head, but smiled softly and took a deep breath.

"During the voyage," the old man began to say, "the princess, Aurelia, befriended a woman who was the medicine woman for the king and his soldiers. She would heal any of the men who would be wounded in battle. Aurelia told the medicine woman that she was in love with the young warrior, Kristian. The king did not know that the young couple had made plans to run away and start a new life. The medicine woman gave Aurelia a medallion. A very powerful and magical gemstone. With it, the medicine woman said, Aurelia would be able to hide from the king in the lake and then escape with Kristian."

"So what happened next?" Sam gulped.

"As soon as Aurelia went into the water, her legs turned into a tail and she was unable to leave," Mr. Brown said, staring deep into Sam's eyes. "We all have to be very careful in whom we place our trust."

"Okay," Sam said.

Mr. Brown raised his eyebrows. "'Okay?' That's all you have to say when I tell you this woman turned into a mermaid?"

Sam frowned, thinking quickly. "Well... uh, you've told me some crazy things so far. I'm just, you know, going with it."

"Hmm," Mr. Brown answered, a smile playing at his lips.

"Plus," Sam added, remembering, "I already know that Mr. Fisher believes there's a mermaid in Moon Lake. And he's looking for a... medallion."

"Yes. Mr. Fisher. His heart is in the right place even if he doesn't know the whole story. But, I suppose, who does? Unfortunately, I believe the Fishers will have a part to play in all of this before it is over. As will you. And I. And... others." Mr. Brown nodded toward the door.

"And who?" Sam asked. "That nurse?"

Mr. Brown bowed his head and sighed. Then he continued, back to his story. "The medicine woman never told Aurelia she would transform. But she did promise that Kristian would come to her. That wasn't a lie. But Kristian was unable to understand the mermaid's speech. And Aurelia immediately grew incredibly powerful. More powerful than the medicine woman or the king ever imagined. She also suffered a dark and terrible change in her mind. In a very real way, the girl Aurelia was gone. What was left in her place was something infinitely dangerous. And vengeful. Evil does exist, Sam. Even the most pure and beautiful among us can be transformed. Such is the power of that medallion. King Gerald never had the chance to kill Kristian. In her rage, Aurelia unleashed her wrath on the Viking ships. All but one were sunk. Kristian's ship was spared. But, according to the legend, not all the Vikings on those sunken ships were killed."

"Wait," Sam said excitedly, "for real?"

"Very real. Unknown to the mermaid, about twenty Vikings made it to shore. They retreated to the hills, built a hidden community, and survived. My people and theirs have kept a delicate peace ever since."

Sam's mind whirled. Aurelia didn't know that some Vikings had survived. And their ancestors were still around?

"Without the medallion, the mermaid's powers are greatly diminished. But every one hundred years, on the anniversary of her transformation, under the light of the full moon, Aurelia becomes so powerful that she has a chance to escape the lake forever."

Sam stared at the older man. Mr. Brown looked so old and tired that Sam almost believed he was indeed one hundred and twenty years old.

"Mr. Brown?" Sam asked softly. "How do you know all this?"

Mr. Brown's hand reached up to his face. With a finger, he traced the line of his deep scar from his forehead, all the way down to his neck.

Even though Mr. Brown was weak and, according to what he had said, close to death, when he raised his eyes to Sam's, there was great power in them. "I was there one hundred years ago. The battle was fierce. This time... this time I'm not sure I will be able to control her."

"There you are, Sam!"

Sam turned to see his father in the doorway.

"Mr. Brown," Sam's dad said, concerned. "I heard you were here. How are you?"

Mr. Brown smiled. "I've been better, sheriff. Then again, I've been worse."

Mr. Lawrence nodded, knowingly. "Sam, you won't believe it, but we're here to bring Leah home! The doctors can't explain it but she's healing at such an incredible rate. No one knows why but—who cares! It's a miracle!"

Sam jumped to his feet.

"Really?!"

All the darkness Sam had been feeling—disappeared at once. He ran to his father and gave him a huge hug.

"Whoa, the ribs, watch the ribs!" Mr. Lawrence laughed. "Come on, she's ready to go. Mr. Brown, let us know if there's anything we can do."

Mr. Brown smiled, but at Sam, "I will."

As Sam followed his father out the door, Mr. Brown called to him.

"Young Warrior?"

Sam turned slowly, still feeling guilty for not sharing everything he knew with Mr. Brown.

"All that glitters is not gold. Remember. Be careful in whom you place your trust."

CHAPTER TWENTY-FIVE

Changes

A few days later, Sam caught himself as he stood quietly outside Leah's closed door. It was surprisingly quiet. Leah always had music blaring. Now, Sam strained to hear any sign of life at all.

During the drive home from the hospital, Leah had been talkative and lively. She was almost bouncing up and down with energy. She and Sam's mom had chatted endlessly, as if nothing had changed, as if Leah hadn't even been in the hospital with life-threatening injuries at all. Mr. Lawrence had spent most of the trip glancing at Leah in the rearview mirror and grinning ear to ear. Sam had even seen his father wipe a tear from his eye.

No one had mentioned the miracle of Leah's recovery. It was as if no one wanted to break the spell or jinx it by mentioning it. Leah was safe, and that was what mattered. Still, Sam had sneaked more than a few looks at his sister out of the corner of his eye as he sat next to her in the backseat. She kept raising her hand to her chest and—Sam knew—caressing the medallion that was tucked under her blouse.

On the way, Leah had asked if they could stop by a beauty salon so she could buy something. Sam's parents were more than happy to do it.

Once they were home, Leah had gone straight to her room and Sam's parents had sat down on the couch to watch TV—like nothing had even happened.

Sam knew this was exactly what everyone needed, to slip back into normal mode and try to forget about the agonizing ups and downs of the past few days. But still, it felt weird.

Sam knew he had to talk to Aurelia after all the negative and mysterious things Mr. Brown had said about her. But first, he felt the need to talk to Leah about the medallion.

Sam opened Leah's door an inch. When he peeked through the cracked door, he noticed a girl with bleach blonde hair staring into the full-length mirror attached to the wall. She was holding her new bottle of hair dye in one hand and caressing the medallion in the other. Her fingers looked bony and her fingernails were long and painted black.

"Leah?" Sam asked. He could barely recognize his sister. Her face looked different. It seemed longer somehow, and the angles of her cheekbones seemed sharper. Then there was the hair color, so bleach blonde that it was nearly white.

"Yes, Sam?" Leah responded slowly, not even glancing at her brother. Normally, Leah would yell at Sam for opening her door unannounced. But now she just continued staring into the mirror, as if getting used to her own body for the first time.

Whoa, Sam thought, *am I crazy or did her voice just sound like Aurelia's? And her eyes... it's like they're glowing...*

"What can I do for you, my dear little munchkin?" Her voice sounded cold and distant.

"Uh," Sam scratched his head, wondering where to start. "Nice hair. You said you'd never go blonde."

"Things change," Leah whispered to herself in the mirror. Then she effortlessly swung her long blonde-white hair over her shoulder and turned her head, slowly to look at Sam. Her brown eyes glowed with electricity. "A lot needs to change, actually. I'm a bit over the *old me*."

The way she said "old me" made Sam feel goosebumps all over his body. At that moment, an eerie feeling filled the room. The medallion around Leah's neck pulsed with a dark blue-green glow. Leah gasped and placed her hand on her heart.

"I feel so weird, Sam," she croaked. Leah suddenly let out an ear-piercing scream, hugging her body as if she was freezing cold, and started trembling.

"Leah? Leah!" their mother's concerned voice pierced the room. And then, just as quickly as it had started, Leah's screaming stopped. She crumpled onto her bed and started whispering.

"Viking blood," she hissed with a dead stare in her eyes. "Viking blood, Viking blood," she repeated, as if chanting.

Then Leah suddenly leapt up and ripped her full-length mirror right off the wall. It hit the floor and shattered into a hundred pieces. Leah marched right up into Sam's face and then dug her long black fingernails into Sam's hand.

"Ow! Quit it!" Sam yelled. But her claws dug even deeper. Through the pain, Sam gaped down and saw deep blue veins running down Leah's arm. Her forearms looked thin, like the bones of a bird. In shock, Sam registered that his sister looked like a starvation victim. Sam shook his hand violently and finally broke her grip just as his mother and father rushed into the room.

Sam followed their eyes down to the shattered glass. Somehow, Leah's whole makeup table was flipped on its side, its contents scattered across the floor.

"What is going on in here?" Mr. Lawrence demanded.

"It was him," Leah hissed. "Look what he did!"

"What?" Sam's eyes bulged. "What are you talking about? I didn't do that!"

"Yes, you did. Don't lie!" Leah was nearly screeching.

"How could you blame this on me?" Sam's eyes revealed the hurt inside. *Why was she lying like this?*

"Sam!" his mother gasped.

"Get out of your sister's room." Mr. Lawrence pointed to the door.

"But—" Sam began.

"Now!" his father bellowed.

Sam left without another word. Leah covered her face with her hands but Sam glanced back and saw the smirk on her lips.

Sam put his back to the wall just outside Leah's room.

"I'm so sorry, Leah," he heard his mom say. "I don't understand why Sam would do that but… it's been a hard time for us all."

"He's jealous," Sam heard his sister say. "He thinks I'm getting all the attention and he doesn't like it."

Outside the door, Sam opened his mouth in a silent scream: *What?!*

"Maybe. Maybe," he heard his father say. "The important thing is that you're home safe. The rest we can figure out."

Sam inched his head past the doorframe and snuck a look back into the room. His mother and father had their backs to him. They were both hugging Leah. Leah's eyes found Sam's immediately. Again, the smirk played across her face and then turned into a sneer as she pulled one corner of her lips up sharply.

***

Sam raced downstairs, straight out the door, and across the street to Alex's house. Sam had called the Fisher's house several times over the past few days, but each time it went to their voicemail. As if Alex and his family had been avoiding him. Sam rushed to the door and knocked. His frantic breathing started to slow. The sun was setting and the streetlights in the neighborhood flickered on.

Just as Mrs. Fisher opened the door, a smoke cloud of incense wafted out. Her smile was genuine and soft. Her words rolled out in her thick accent.

"I hope your family is doing better, now that Leah has returned in good condition." She raised her bejeweled hand and gestured for Sam to come inside the house. "Come in. Alex is playing video games upstairs."

Mrs. Fisher was wearing a long necklace with a large clear crystal pendant and a flowing dress of sapphire velvet. Peaceful music was playing in the background, something folky with violins and mandolins.

Sam didn't step inside.

Mrs. Fisher cocked her head. "Would you like some food?"

When Sam opened his mouth to decline the offer, she spoke again.

"Wait. Let me see your hand."

Sam furrowed his eyebrows, not understanding, but without another word, Mrs. Fisher took both of Sam's hands and turned them over to study his palms.

"Ah," she whispered. "I knew it."

"Huh? Knew what?" Sam looked down at his hands. "What's wrong?"

The marks from Leah's nails! Sam realized. The claw marks were still there, deep red indentations in his palms.

Sam thought fast. "Oh, that's just Geezer, my cat. I was playing with him and he--"

"Hush. The time for lies is over. I saw it in your aura."

Mrs. Fisher finally looked up from Sam's palms and fixed her penetrating eyes on his questioning ones. "You have given the medallion to someone."

"What? No! I mean…"

"I know why you lied to us, Sam. Trust. You cannot force trust. It must be earned. We thought we had the time to earn your trust. But now it seems, we don't."

Sam didn't know what to say. He didn't want to lie, but he didn't want to tell the truth either.

"The Mystical Medallion," Mrs. Fisher whispered. "Do you know what you've done? Now you have unleashed it. You have given it to someone you should not have."

Mrs. Fisher looked back down at Sam's palms. She closed her eyes and breathed deeply, as if inhaling Sam's very aura.

"A woman," she finally declared. "A young woman. Oh no. Wait…"

Sam shivered, but couldn't open his mouth. He felt dumbfounded.

"Uh, I don't know what you're talking about," Sam said nervously. He backed up slowly, one step at a time. Mrs. Fisher lifted her head and opened her eyes. She placed her hands on her hips and tilted her head, studying Sam's face.

"Do you still visit the mermaid? Or was it once? Twice? Tell me, boy. Does she come to you at the lake? Do you hear her in your head? You haven't kissed her, have you?"

Sam didn't dare to look at her eyes directly. He focused on a spot behind her and noticed Alex, at the top of the stairs, peeking his head around the bannister, listening. As soon as he saw Sam, Alex immediately shrank back, out of sight.

Unconsciously, Sam's eyes found Mrs. Fisher's. Her eyes were flashing with energy. Suddenly, Alex's mother seemed taller, stronger, invincible even. And maybe a little bit crazy. Sam backed up and tripped his way down the few steps leading up to the door. He spun around and darted back toward his house. When Sam looked up, he noticed Leah's ashen face and skeleton-white hair in the window. His window. Leah was in Sam's room, spying on him. A harsh frown darkened her face. Her glowing eyes burning into him like laser beams.

Sam stopped in his tracks. He didn't want to face Leah. He didn't understand what was happening to her, nor why Mrs. Fisher was so forceful and mysterious. Without a second thought, Sam raced to the garage and lifted up the door. He jumped on his bike. He knew where he had to go. He also knew now that he had been avoiding it. But he couldn't wait any longer.

Sam streaked out of the garage, not even stopping to close it. He spun his head around, lowered his shoulders, and pedaled as hard as he could. When he braved one last glance at the Fisher's house, he saw that Alex's mom was still staring at him, her hands on her hips.

Then he heard her voice reaching out to him, "Mark my words. You will come back. I only pray it is soon enough."

CHAPTER TWENTY-SIX

The Unknown Truth

By the time Sam got to the spot of the lake where he usually met Aurelia, he collapsed onto the sand. He was out of breath and completely exhausted.

Wow, he thought, *things are really different without the medallion. With it on, nothing could phase me. I never got tired. I never felt afraid.*

It was a creepy thought. He missed the medallion's power, but at the same time, he was also starting to be very afraid of it.

What if Mr. Brown was right? What if the girl, Aurelia, is gone and the creature left in her place is mean? Manipulative. Evil.

"Darling Sam!" The voice sounded like wind chimes dancing in a summer breeze. But somehow, although that voice had always sent a thrill of excitement down Sam's spine, now it just sent a cold shiver.

Involuntarily, Sam jumped to his feet.

"Sammy?" Aurelia giggled. "You look so funny. Like you've seen a ghost." The mermaid spun around, then leapt halfway onto the sand, keeping her tail in the water and swishing it around slowly, methodically. Her eyes followed Sam's every move. She batted her long silver eyelashes and coyly dropped her head to one shoulder.

"Are you here to thank me, my dear?"

"Aurelia?" Sam said, sounding hurt. "What is wrong with my sister?"

Aurelia's mouth slipped open a bit, in surprise. She shook her head side to side just enough for her long beautiful hair to bounce gently on her shoulders. Sam couldn't take his eyes off her.

"What do you mean, my love? Isn't she healed?"

When she smiled, Sam felt it lighten his soul with its simple, all-consuming beauty. He couldn't help but be mesmerized. She was so pretty. She was perfect.

He took a few steps and sat down next to her, gazing at her all the while. Why was he doubting her again? Why would he question her when she helped heal his sister?

All these problems felt far away and even unimportant.

Aurelia reached out and touched Sam's arm. He shivered at how cold her touch was. As if realizing her mistake, Aurelia pulled her hand back.

"Sorry, my Sam. You will notice that, without the medallion, you do not feel so strong, do you? With me it's the same. Without it I feel the cold of the water. I tire when I swim. It was quite a sacrifice I made, offering it to your sister. You see that, don't you?"

Sam swallowed. "Leah is different. She's become cruel. She's lying. I know it sounds strange but she just seems— evil."

Aurelia raised her eyebrows innocently. "Evil? What an interesting thought."

"She isn't who she used to be," Sam continued in distress. "She's not... she doesn't act like my sister anymore. What happened?"

Aurelia's eyes burned deeply into Sam's. It felt like she was looking straight into his soul. The mermaid let out a cloud of mist after she breathed in the cold night air.

"What happened is that we can be together, Sam. Really together. Isn't that what you wanted?"

"Well, yeah, of course. But I don't understand. How does Leah acting completely like someone else mean you and me can be together?"

"Oh Sam!" The mermaid splashed her tail, playfully. "I'm just so happy that you helped me!" Her enchanting voice echoed through Sam's ears.

"You helped me escape the lake!"

Sam's voice squeaked as he shivered in response. "What? But I never helped you with anything like that. What are you talking about?"

"You found my mystical medallion," Aurelia said, dropping her lips into a cute pout. "Since then, you found your way back to me, my little Sam. And now," Aurelia tilted her head back and let out a playful laugh, "now your sister wears the medallion."

This time, when Aurelia laughed, it made Sam feel strange. Not elated or excited or warm, like it always had before. This laugh made him concerned. More than concerned. It made him scared.

Sam spoke slowly. "What does Leah wearing the medallion have to do with you leaving the lake?"

Aurelia slumped just a little. Her lips pressed together as if disappointed that Sam was being so unappreciative. She shook her head.

"You should be happy that I gave her a new life," she said coldly. "Your sister would have died anyway."

"What are you talking about?" Sam shook his head back and forth in denial.

"Don't you see? My medallion made you strong. Powerful. Because you are a man. Well, a boy. I never told you, but if a *woman* wears the medallion, it takes her over completely. Just like it did when I wore it into the lake those hundreds of years ago. When I turned into a mermaid."

"So Leah will turn into a mermaid?"

"No, silly," Aurelia's eyes flashed. "Are you really this dim? Do you really not understand?"

Why is she talking to me like this? This can't be happening. Sam closed his eyes, and wished it was a bad dream. When he did, it felt like he could think clearer. Like, if he wasn't looking at the mermaid, captivated by her beauty, her power over him diminished.

"Little Sam," the mermaid said coldly. "Look at me. Look at me!"

Sam obeyed and opened his eyes.

"I saw your sister before the accident, Sam. At the party. I knew she would be the perfect body to enter. Beautiful, young, and full of life. The same age as me when I was tricked and trapped into this horrible lake. Once the hundred-year anniversary happens and the full moon is at its strongest and brightest, the medallion will reach the crescendo of its power. Tomorrow at midnight... *I will* become your sister!"

Aurelia's voice echoed over the lake.

Sam was in shock. Again, he closed his eyes.

Again, his thoughts became clearer.

Still with his eyes closed, Sam said, "But… you can't do that. She's… she's her own person. What will happen to her?"

"Consider her a passenger. She'll be there, somewhere. Deep down. She'll be completely powerless but she'll have, shall we say, a window onto the world. My world. If I let her… If she behaves."

Sam couldn't believe his ears. Without even thinking, he then said, "But how can you say that you and me will be together if…"

"If what? If I'm your sister?" Aurelia smirked. "Oh please, Sam. You played your part. Don't you see? We will be together. You'll be my little brother. Ha! Did you really think I would be your *girlfriend*?" Her laugh came out like a hiss. "I'm three hundred and sixteen years old. You're what, fourteen? Sorry, Sammy, but that's an age difference I just can't get over."

Sam couldn't help but open his eyes to look at her. He was hurt. The sideways smile on Aurelia's face was full of bitterness and scorn.

The mermaid laughed and the sound felt like it was piercing Sam's brain. He covered his ears with his hands. He hated everything that was happening. He felt betrayed. He felt dumb for even believing her.

"You used me," Sam shouted. He couldn't hold back the tears that watered his eyes.

Aurelia sat up tall and started shouting at the world. "I can finally escape this wretched pool of water and there is nothing… *nothing* you can do about it! Any of you!"

Aurelia spread her arms, as if she could embrace the night. Then she pushed herself off the sand and dove straight into the cold water of the lake. A few icy drops splashed on Sam's skin. He watched her luminous tail grow dim as it disappeared into the murky waters.

The ripples from the water calmed.

The wind grew still.

Dark clouds slowly covered the bright, nearly-full moon, leaving Moon Lake to a silent black night.

Sam sat, blinking at the calm, dark water. It had all been a lie. She was never interested in him — like that.

Mr. Brown had been right.

The Fishers had been right.

They had been right about everything.

But one thought pushed all the others out of Sam's mind.

Leah.

I have to save Leah!

CHAPTER TWENTY-SEVEN

Preparations

"Mr. Brown! Mr. Brown! Mr…"

Sam wasn't expecting to see what he saw when, out of breath from the bike ride, he burst into the hospital room.

Sam was ready to share everything with the older man. No more secrets. Mr. Brown had proven himself to be one hundred percent worthy of Sam's trust. Unlike Aurelia. His greatest hope for Leah was Mr. Brown. Surely he knew how Sam could save his sister.

But as Sam quietly took in the sight in the hospital room, his hopes were dashed. In their place was a deep, dark, yawning pit in his stomach.

Mr. Brown's face was ashen gray. For the first time, he truly looked one hundred and twenty years old. Tubes ran from Mr. Brown's arms, connected to big, new medical machines that now occupied half the room.

"Coma," came the quiet voice behind Sam.

Sam turned to see the older, angelic-faced nurse standing next to him.

"It was very peaceful. And unique. What he said…"

Her voice trailed off, in concern.

"What?" Sam breathed. "What did he say?"

The nurse turned her bright blue eyes on Sam.

"He said, 'I must go. I must prepare.' And then he slipped away."

Sam turned back to his friend, hoping for any sign of life.

"Prepare?" Sam whispered to himself.

"Sam," the older woman said. "You'd better go. You have some preparing to do, yourself."

"But... where? How?"

The nurse nodded toward Mr. Brown. "Don't count him out."

"I thought you just said he's in a coma. Will he come out of it?"

The nurse sighed. "By the time the sun rises again, he will arise—or he won't."

Sam blinked at her. He felt a lump in his throat.

"Believe me. He can still help. And he will."

Sam shook his head, not understanding.

The nurse placed her hand on Sam's shoulder. "You must go. Now. Your sister needs you most of all."

***

When Sam arrived on his street again, he didn't even look over at his house. He didn't want to see Leah, and somehow he didn't want her to see him either.

Sam burst right through the front door of the Fisher's residence. He didn't bother ringing the doorbell. The living room still stunk of incense.

The sound of meditation music tinkled in the background. Mrs. Fisher, unsurprised by Sam's entrance, was sitting quietly on the couch reading an old book.

"Upstairs," was all she said.

Sam ran up the stairs, two steps at a time. He heard voices coming from the room opposite Alex's—Mr. Fisher's office. He raced straight in.

Sitting at the desk, Alex and Mr. Fisher both looked up at him. The dull glow of the large computer monitor painted their faces in a pale, blue light. The desk was covered in messy stacks of disorganized papers and electrical wires snaking from the computer. Mr. Fisher immediately rummaged through the papers and grabbed a book.

"You are in grave danger," Mr. Fisher said. He started flipping through pages of the book. It looked ancient.

"You must tell me," Mr. Fisher continued, "This is very crucial." He studied Sam's face through his large glasses. "I know that you gave the medallion to someone. Was it your sister, Leah?"

Sam nodded.

Mr. Fisher slid the book in front of Sam. He traced his fingers over a gory scene of corpses being devoured by evil mermaid creatures.

Mr. Fisher sighed. "Sirens. Beautiful, yet dangerous creatures. They lure sailors with their enchanting voices to their death. Look, it even says that the mermaids absorb the energy, the life spirit, of whoever wears the medallion. At the right time, their souls can even leave their bodies to enter another."

"Yeah," Sam said, feeling sick in his stomach. "She told me."

"She told you?!" Alex and his father said at once.

Sam felt dizzy and pushed the book with its grisly images back away from him. But Mr. Fisher shoved it right into Sam's face.

"That's how they lure you in. The Sirens poison the mind with love stories and love songs. And if you let them kiss you... you will do whatever they ask of you and you will be happy to do so." The painted illustration showed another mermaid sitting on a rock with her arms wrapped around a helpless sailor. Sam snatched the book from Mr. Fisher's hands and threw it on the ground. The book slid across the floor and thudded against the wall.

Sam turned away. "I know I lied to you. Both of you. And I'm sorry. I didn't want to believe it. I thought she... I thought she..."

"Loved you," Mr. Fisher finished.

Sam stared down at the ground, his face flushed with pain and hopelessness. Mr. Fisher stood and gently pushed Sam down into his chair.

"Look, I'm a scientist. I have studied this kind of research for more years than you have lived on Earth."

Mr. Fisher gave Alex a look, then turned back to Sam. "I think you know by now that the mermaid in Moon Lake is looking for a way to escape. She's been trapped for many years."

"Three hundred to be exact," Sam said slowly.

"Yes, Sam, three hundred years. Or… according to my calculations, approximately three hours from now. I believe the mermaid is using the medallion to escape from the lake."

"It's Leah," Sam interrupted. "It's my sister. Aurelia's going to possess her body. Leah will be like a passenger. At best."

Alex and his father exchanged a surprised look.

"You know all this?" Alex asked.

Sam was tearing up. "It's all my fault. I thought Mr. Brown could help. But now he's in a coma. I don't know what to do. He was my only hope. He knows so much."

"So do we," Mrs. Fisher said from the doorway.

***

Alex's father whipped the black sheet off the large rectangular object like a magician finishing a trick. Sam hadn't noticed the huge shape behind him in the room before. Now it was revealed.

It was a cage. The bars were shining silver. It was still on the same wheels that Sam had seen that night so long ago when he had watched Mr. Fisher push it into the house.

"Silver," Alex said.

"Viking silver," Mr. Fisher added.

"Ancient Viking silver," Mrs. Fisher corrected. He stared at the cage like it was his prized possession.

"It took a lifetime of searching to find enough of it to smelt down and make this. There's nothing like it in the world."

Alex touched Sam on the shoulder. "Leah has the medallion now?"

Sam nodded.

"Is she at home?" Alex added.

"I don't know," Sam admitted.

Alex's mother shook her head. "She is not. I saw her leave just before you came. By now she will be at the lake."

"Then we have to go!" Sam jumped up. "We can take her, the three of us. We can hold her down and…"

"No," Alex's mom said. "It's not that simple. The medallion works with women in a specific way. As soon as it begins working, it creates an attachment. It must be completely destroyed, in a very specific way. If not, Leah will die." Mrs. Fisher's words terrified Sam.

"What do you mean, specifically?"

"Look," Alex's dad said. He picked up the ancient book off the floor and flipped to another page.

There was an image of a mermaid bursting out of the ocean, twisted up in obvious agony. On a nearby rowboat were an unconscious young woman, and a Viking sailor holding her hand.

With his other hand, the sailor was stabbing a medallion much like Aurelia's with a bright, silver knife. His mouth was open and, surrounding him, were handwritten words in a strange language.

"Viking silver again," said Mr. Fisher. "Only Viking silver will penetrate the medallion. And the one who destroys the medallion must do it while the enchanted words are said by a person of great magical blood." Mr. Fisher pointed to the strange writings. "You see, very specific."

Sam's mind was whirling. He needed a Viking silver weapon. He had to say...

"But I can't read those words."

"I can," Mrs. Fisher said, rising to her full height. She nodded to Alex, "All in my family learn the languages of power."

"The words don't need to be said by the man who was enchanted," Alex added.

"And my side of the family is Scandinavian," Mr. Fisher said. "Which means we have Viking blood. And one more piece of Viking silver that has been passed through the generations."

Mr. Fisher swung open a wardrobe cabinet. But it was not exactly full of clothes. Sam exhaled in a whistle.

Knives, maces, swords, and other shiny weapons were hanging inside. Most looked hundreds of years old. Sam reached out to a gleaming long knife.

"Viking silver?"

"No," Mr. Fisher said. "The shiniest is not always the best. Here. My great grandfather gave me this."

Mr. Fisher picked up an old battle-axe. It was only a little bigger than a hatchet. Mr. Fisher handed it to Sam. It was surprisingly heavy. Its shaft was old, notched wood covered in the scars of battle. The head of it was so old and stained that it looked completely dull and neglected. Sam could see chips missing from the blade. He shook his head.

"But this..." Sam started, not wanting to seem unthankful or insulting. "This axe seems a little... dull."

Behind the thick glasses, Mr. Fisher's eyes blinked in confusion.

"Dull?"

He took the axe from Sam and, in one movement, turned and swiped it downward. To Sam's surprise, the blade passed straight through the huge computer monitor, then straight through the wooden desk, itself. Electric sparks flew from the monitor as it and the desk fell apart, crashing to the ground, each in two clean pieces.

"Oi," Mrs. Fisher said. "You couldn't have demonstrated it on something cheaper?"

Mr. Fisher smiled sheepishly. Sam stared in awe for a moment. Then he lowered his head.

"I'm so sorry for not trusting you," he said, looking to the floor in embarrassment.

"We know," Alex said. "We're used to it. We're not the average family. And we look a little..."

"Odd?" Mrs. Fisher said, completing her son's sentence.

"Creepy?" Mr. Fisher said, raising his hands like werewolf claws. Alex covered his eyes and shook his head.

"What? Isn't that a word you kids use?" Mr. Fisher chuckled.

"Well," Sam said, "looks can be deceiving."

Mrs. Fisher smiled at him. "Yes, dear Sam. Yes, they can."

"Yeah but..." Sam shook his head. "Why are you helping me?"

"It's my life's work," Mr. Fisher said.

"And it's the right thing to do," Mrs. Fisher said in support.

"But mostly," Alex said, stepping closer to Sam, "because you're our friend."

Sam suddenly threw his arms around all three of them. After a moment, he pulled back, wiping at his eyes.

"Okay," Sam said with a heavy exhale. "Mrs. Fisher chants while I hold Leah and somehow use this thing on the medallion. I got it. Let's go." Sam turned to the door.

"Wait," Alex said.

"Aren't you forgetting something?" Mr. Fisher said, pointing down at the image of the agonized mermaid in the book.

Alex nodded. "She won't exactly stand by as we do this."

"And she will be at the apex of her power," Mrs. Fisher said ominously.

Sam closed his eyes. "Right. Right. Okay, so… what else do we need?"

Alex's eyes narrowed. A powerful grin pulled at the corner of his mouth. Sam could hardly believe it, but Alex actually looked — dangerous…

"We need a plan."

CHAPTER TWENTY-EIGHT

Unleashed

Sam had made straight for the same spot where he and Aurelia had met several times before and sure enough, his sister was there.

The night was still.

The sky was cloudless and Leah stood motionless at the edge of the lake.

Above them, the full moon illuminated a thick blanket of fog covering the cold, deep waters of Moon Lake. Sam had never seen the moon look so bright and large. He could even make out the individual craters on the moon's surface.

Leah had her back to him, so he could not tell if she would notice his approach. Sam tiptoed off the path, but as soon as he did, the sticks and leaves started crackling under his feet. He stopped and held his breath. A loud splash startled him.

Over the lake's surface, the mermaid's head and shoulders slowly emerged out of the fog. Sam froze. Even though Leah didn't notice his presence — Aurelia knew he was there. From the distance, Sam could not see Aurelia's face clearly but her skin had a murky, green hue rather than its usual gentle blue. Her arms and chest seemed oily. Sam saw the moonlight reflect off her arms and noticed that, like her tail, Aurelia's arms now seemed to be covered in scales. She beckoned Leah with a wave and Sam's sister immediately started wading out into the lake.

"No!" Sam shouted.

There was no sense trying to be quiet now.

"Leah! Leah!" Sam shouted as he ran towards his sister. Leah stopped just as the water reached her chest, ten yards into the lake. Sam's feet splashed into the icy water and he felt a chill race up his spine. Before he reached her, though, Sam saw a glistening shape race under the water like a torpedo. It circled Leah, then sped right towards him. At the last moment, the underwater shape veered off and just missed colliding with him.

An electric jolt of agony rocked Sam's body, throwing him backward, into the water. He shouted in pain. He had felt something like a lion's claw rip into his leg and knew immediately that Aurelia had scraped him with her long fingernails. Sam scrambled up onto the sand.

He sat, panting at the water's edge, gaping down at his pants, shredded at the knee, and the four long gashes in his leg. Blood was already flowing from them.

"Sam." The voice twisted across the surface of the lake like the hiss of a bottom-dwelling sea serpent. "Sam," it repeated, "why have you come?"

Sam looked up. In front of him, Aurelia was halfway out of the water. Sam gasped when he caught full sight of Aurelia's face for the first time in the moonlight. It was no longer beautiful. In fact, it was terrifying. He saw sickly looking green scales on her face. Her hair, normally silver and shining, was now grey and ragged. And what used to be full, pink lips had now turned into thin, black cracks. They were pulled back, revealing sharp teeth whose only purpose was to tear flesh and bite through bone.

"What's the matter?" Aurelia teased in her husky, serpent's voice. "Don't you think I'm still pretty?" The way she snarled sent more shivers up Sam's spine.

"Aurelia," Sam said, mustering his courage and involuntarily inching backwards. "Why are you doing this? There must be another way."

"Foolish boy," the mermaid hissed. "This *is* the only way. Your sister will be mine tonight. If you know what's good for you, you'll play along… Forever."

Sam's blood froze when he heard the word, *forever*.

"But that's not fair," he squeaked helplessly. "Leah doesn't want this."

The mermaid was shaking with anger and waves of water rippled around her.

"Fair?!" the mermaid raged. "Was it fair for me to be imprisoned here for three hundred years without my love? Don't you dare speak to me about fairness!"

It's working, Sam thought. *She's taking the bait.*

From the corner of his eye, he saw Alex and Ethan inching toward Aurelia from their hiding spots in the bushes. As planned, they had made their way to the shoreline secretly and were sneaking towards Aurelia just out of her vision. Alex and Ethan each carried a long canoe oar.

They're getting closer, Sam thought. *Keep her talking, distracted from her senses.*

"You win," he said, summoning a crack in his voice as if he was terrified of Aurelia in all her predatory glory. "But please, can I just say goodbye to my sister?"

The mermaid cocked her head, considering. Sam knew what was going through her mind though. Was Sam tricking her? Half of her mouth now pulled upwards into a sneer.

"Goodbye?" she cackled. "How pathetic. I already told you. I will share her body with her, as one person. She will still be in there... well, if she's a good girl."

Suddenly Alex yelled, "Now!"

Ethan and Alex both lunged out of the forest, swinging their oars back and forth towards Aurelia. When Aurelia saw this, she immediately turned away from Sam and focused all of her attention on Alex and Ethan. Both boys sliced their canoe oars through the air. The mermaid screeched.

With Aurelia now distracted, Sam knew this was his only chance to save Leah. With every muscle in his body, he ran through the shallow water as fast as he could. The water was up to his knees as Sam grabbed Leah's shoulder, spun her around — and then stopped for a moment when he saw her face.

Leah's face looked angelic. Peaceful. Enchanted.

Her eyes seemed to gaze straight through her brother. Not recognizing him or anything else. She was under Aurelia's spell.

Sam hugged his sister, then began to pull her towards the shoreline. With one final shove, he pushed Leah onto the sand. Leah fell to her knees, still in her dreamlike state of mind, as if nothing had happened.

Sam heard the words, "Watch out!" echo over the lake.

Just as Sam turned around to see what was happening with his friends, a terrible pain shot straight through his leg.

It felt like his entire foot had no more blood flowing through it. He realized Aurelia's claw-like fingers were now clenched around his ankle, squeezing tightly. The mermaid's face twisted in rage. With one mighty yank, she dragged Sam into the depths of the icy water.

Ethan and Alex both yelled and started running towards Sam, but they were too late.

***

Underwater, Sam was being pulled at an incredible speed. Aurelia's grip on his ankle felt like it was burning through his bones. It all happened so fast. Water shot up his nose, causing Sam to gasp and choke underwater, forcing all of the air out of his lungs.

Deeper and deeper they went, faster and faster. Sam closed his eyes and resisted the urge to open his mouth for air. He knew all he would get was a lungful of water. Sam tried to fight Aurelia's strong pull, but there was no point. She tightened her grip.

Sam's chest burned as every cell in his body cried out for oxygen.

This is the end. I can't fight back, Sam thought as he exhaled his last breath of air. He began to let himself go, accepting the fact that the mermaid would drown him until his death.

The world turned slow-motion. Sam visualized every last detail of the water bubbles around him.

It was a beautiful sight in such a horrifying moment, the mystical glow of Aurelia's tail reflected through the bubbles with the colors of blue, green and purple.

Just then, Sam was hit with a burst of oxygen as he was thrown against the rocks. The mermaid had brought him back to her underwater cave. Sam collapsed onto his stomach, panting for air.

"Sam," the word slithered off the walls in ghastly echoes.

He lifted himself to his knees and turned to see Aurelia's head in the water a few feet from him. She was terrifying to behold.

"You've betrayed me," the mermaid said, slowly rising out of the water.

"Me?" Sam let out, still gasping for air. "I betrayed you? You're out of your mind."

Aurelia smashed her tail onto the surface, causing a deluge of water to pour over Sam.

"Don't fight me. Join me or there will be consequences."

Sam stood up on wobbly legs.

He stared into Aurelia's glowing green eyes.

"Aurelia. This isn't you. Not the real you. This is the curse. What happened to you was terrible. It was unfair and tragic. But possessing my sister's body and turning her into your mental prisoner? You'd be doing to her what the Viking medicine woman did to you. Is that what you want?"

Sam's voice echoed off the high walls and ceiling. Aurelia blinked as she drifted closer to the shore of the cave. It was as if Sam saw a flicker of regret pass over the mermaid's face.

She had been so beautiful, Sam thought. *And now look at her.*

Sam could see greenish scales on the mermaid's face in detail. Her entire facial structure looked rugged and worn down.

Sam pressed on. "Tell me the sweet, loving Aurelia still exists somewhere in there."

"She's here, Sam." A tear trickled down Aurelia's face, "She's still here."

"Then let's work this out. I want to help you."

Aurelia was shaking her head in regret. "If you really want to help me, let me have Leah. It's the only way."

"No, we'll find another way. I have friends who can help. They know things."

Aurelia kept shaking her head. Then the look on her face turned slowly from regret into disgust.

"There is no other way."

Aurelia bared her fangs and leapt out of the water, landing on Sam as she declared, inches from his face, "And if you won't help me... *you will die!*"

Her breath was toxic and stung Sam's eyes like pepper spray. Sam tried escaping her grasp, screaming in pain. The mermaid grabbed his arm and before Sam knew it, he was being pulled back through the water. The rocks of the underwater tunnel bashed against his body.

He felt himself being pulled upward and very quickly, his head broke the surface and he was treading water in the middle of the lake. He looked around frantically.

On the shoreline, he could see Ethan and Alex, scanning the surface of the lake, calling out his name.

Aurelia's head suddenly popped up in the water, between Sam and his friends.

"This is your last chance, Sam," she said, closing her eyes. Sam saw the concentration on her face. Incredibly, Aurelia's face morphed back into the one Sam knew well. The beautiful one. The one he had fallen in love with. The gentle, youthful face with long, silver hair. Sam felt his heart tug in his chest as if it wanted to leap from his body and into her hands. Beneath their long lashes, Aurelia's eyes opened. Sam had never seen a more enchanting shade of sparkling green-blue.

"Sam," Aurelia whispered in her old, sweet voice. It sounded like wind chimes jingling daintily in Sam's ears. "Don't you love me anymore?"

The look of sadness on the mermaid's face nearly broke Sam's heart.

"Yes, I fell in love with you," Sam said with genuine concern and affection. "But I'm not sure I should have. I'm not sure I've ever known the real you."

A dark look passed over Aurelia's face, then was gone in an instant.

"You know I can do this with or without you, Sam. But I like you. I really do. I'd rather live with you as my little brother... than drown you right here and now."

Sam gulped.

He ventured a look over Aurelia's head. His friends were nowhere to be seen. That meant their part of the plan was ready. Sam took a deep breath and focused on Aurelia again.

"You can't have my sister. You just can't."

Aurelia drifted closer to Sam, hurt and frailty in her eyes. She reached out to him and, with a long, elegant finger, traced the shape of Sam's cheek. Then her look turned dark. The finger turned green and scaly, then extended into a razor-sharp claw.

In a flash, Aurelia's face flipped back to its green, scaly, true form. Instinctively, Sam jolted backwards with the mermaid's sudden transformation.

Aurelia's eyes registered his disgust and she screeched, "You shall die!"

At that moment, Aurelia grabbed Sam by the hair and pulled him down.

Under the water, Aurelia wrapped her body and tail around Sam, slowly descending.

He tried to fight, but his arms were pinned by her arms, his legs pinned by her tail.

Sam wriggled and fought with everything he had, but the mermaid was just too strong. Her piercing eyes stared into Sam's, as if eager to register the moment of his death. A sneer of hate pulled her lips back, revealing the fangs. She constricted her body around Sam, like a boa.

Sam felt the air leaving his lips. He couldn't help it. Aurelia was literally squeezing the life out of him. Strangely calm, Sam stopped struggling and stared into her eyes. He saw nothing in her but hate and pain. Sam blinked.

He suddenly felt sorry for her. Sorry for the tragic end to her love story, sorry for the curse that had changed her forever — and sorry for her madness.

A smile of recognition suddenly formed on Sam's lips....
An idea.
Sam leaned forward and — kissed her.

Aurelia blinked in shock. Her body slackened its grip for a moment. And in that moment, during the kiss, Sam felt his lungs fill with air.

The mermaid's kiss had, like before, filled him with oxygen. Even if she hadn't intended it, it had worked.

Realizing what was happening, Aurelia pulled back, breaking the connection of their lips, but it was too late. In the split second of confusion, while Aurelia's guard was down just for a moment, Sam acted. He kicked both feet with every last bit of strength he had. Aurelia's eyes went wide in confusion and Sam felt her body fall away from his. He didn't have a moment to lose.

Sam swam as fast as he could for shore. He only had seconds until Aurelia would recover from the shock and pain. Sam swam like he'd never swum before.

On the sand, Ethan and Alex were yelling.

"Hurry!" Ethan cried.

"Behind you!" Alex bellowed. "She's coming!"

Sam didn't allow himself to turn around. He pushed even harder, knowing that he was swimming for his life. If she caught him, he wouldn't get another chance. She would drown him for sure.

He was almost there. The shore was approaching. He heard the waters behind him roiling as Aurelia raced, underwater, toward him.

Sam's stomach scraped the sand. He was almost out of the water! Alex and Ethan were there, up to their ankles in the lake. Both boys pulled Sam to his feet.

"You're alive!" Ethan shouted in relief.

At that moment, Aurelia exploded out of the water, tumbling on the shore. The boys stared in shock as the mermaid lifted her tail and began to crawl on the sand using her hands.

"Run!" Alex yelled. The boys split up, sprinting in different directions.

The mermaid peeled off after Sam, crawling as fast as Sam could run. She dragged herself by the hands, with her tail arched up behind her like some kind of scaly, giant scorpion.

Wait, Sam realized, *she's not coming for me.*

Ahead of him, Sam saw Leah sitting on the sand, under the mermaid's spell, oblivious to everything going on around her. The medallion sparkled on her chest.

Sam ran as fast as he could to reach Leah first. Without breaking stride, Sam yanked the medallion from her neck and kept running. Behind him, he heard the mermaid screech in frustration.

"No!" Aurelia screamed. "Give it back!"

Sam spun and started running for the tree line. Aurelia followed, letting nothing get in her way. The sand turned to pebbles, then the pebbles turned to grass. It didn't slow Aurelia down, but Sam knew exactly where to run. The plan was coming together.

The gashes in his ankle burned with pain, but Sam ignored it. He smashed through tree branches and short, prickly bushes. She was gaining on him, now only mere steps behind him, crashing through the vegetation just like him, but Sam finally felt solid bars beneath his feet. Aurelia was inches behind him now and reached out with her claws. Sam jumped the last few feet and as he did, a wall of silver bars rose up behind him, blocking Aurelia's path.

With a CLANK, Mr. Fisher locked the silver cage door. Aurelia realized that the boy had brought her straight into their trap. The mermaid's ear-piercing scream echoed through the forest.

Ethan and Alex ran up, pulling Leah between them. Alex was holding the Viking hatchet. Aurelia bashed at the doors of the cage, trying to break through.

"Forget it, siren," Mr. Fisher said proudly, panting and beaming at the same time. "Viking silver."

Aurelia hissed, "You and your disgusting Viking spawn will die like the rest."

Alex gulped. Sam didn't waste any time though. Since the medallion was detached from his sister's neck, he only had a matter of time before Leah would be lost in the spell forever. He grabbed the hatchet from Alex, took Leah by the hand, and turned to Aurelia.

"I didn't want to do this," Sam said.

"Well… I want to do *this*," Aurelia said as she began mumbling words in some kind of an eerie melody.

No one had noticed Ethan silently walk behind the cage. He moved stiffly and didn't blink. Not even thinking and in a strange trance, Ethan unbolted the cage.

"No!" Mr. and Mrs. Fisher gasped.

Aurelia grinned, evilly. "Yes."

The silver door clanged to the ground, busting open. Aurelia was filled with rage. She pulled herself from the cage and immediately turned her full force on the closest human. It was Mrs. Fisher. Aurelia reared up and raised her claw, but Mrs. Fisher started chanting. The mermaid's hand stopped mere inches from Mrs. Fisher's face. Aurelia struggled, as if pushing at some invisible force field, before giving up.

"Ah! Gypsy witch!" Aurelia hissed.

She threw herself at the next person — Mr. Fisher. He grabbed his Viking sword just in time to defend himself. The mermaid screamed in pain as her shoulder was stabbed.

In that moment though, Mr. Fisher also felt the impact as the mermaid's claw slashed across his face and neck, the wound pulsing with blood. Immediately, Alex ran to his father. Aurelia thrashed about on the ground for a moment, then shook off her own injury.

Ethan was still under the trance.

Alex and his father were down.

The cage had failed.

Mrs. Fisher was lost in her chanting, eyes closed.

It was up to Sam.

CHAPTER TWENTY-NINE

The Final Battle

Sam tightened his grip on the Viking hatchet, raising it in the air. In the other hand, was the medallion. He knew his mission was to destroy the medallion once and for all.

Just before Sam swung the hatchet down, a clawed hand smashed his face mercilessly. With this hit, the mermaid knocked the air out of Sam. He dropped the hatchet and covered his face in pain. Dazed, Sam's world spun out of focus for a moment. He felt the wounds on his face pulsing. With each surge of his blood, the pain intensified. When he finally looked at his palm, a puddle of blood leaked through his fingers. He slowly looked up and regained his focus. Aurelia slithered towards him victoriously.

This was the moment, Sam realized. Aurelia had won. Her enemies were defeated. The medallion was around her neck. The moon was at its fullest point and Leah was ready to be overtaken. One last act of vengeance and she would possess Leah completely and forever. Aurelia pinned Sam to the ground with one powerful arm.

She looked down into his face and grinned. There was nothing Sam could do. It was really over.

"Silly boy. You've lost."

Aurelia raised her hand over her head, ready to strike.

Sam glanced over at Leah.

It was his last thought. He had failed to save his own sister. He sighed and stared into Aurelia's eyes, ready for the blow to come.

Just as Aurelia was about to swing her claw down at Sam's face, a high-pitched cry came from above, startling Aurelia. She frantically turned to find the source of the screech. Something from above began attacking her from all sides.

It was a blur to Sam, all action and fury, until a few feathers floated down to his face. *Feathers*, Sam thought, *It's Sagitta!*

The hawk collided with the mermaid in a flurry of talons, swiping at her face and then dancing in the air just out of reach of her claws. Sagitta hovered in midair.

"Young warrior." The familiar voice was inside Sam's head. It sounded like Mr. Brown's voice.

"Young warrior," the voice repeated, *"Do what must be done. Do not hesitate."*

Suddenly, Aurelia ripped the medallion off her own chest and swiped up mightily at Sagitta. There was a sickening cracking sound and a bright flash of green. Sam saw Sagitta hurtle through the air, backwards. The bird hit the ground a full thirty feet away, hard, rolling to a stop, unconscious. Her wing was bent behind her at a terrible angle, obviously broken.

"Stop!" Sam shouted.

Aurelia was spread out on the ground, panting and exhausted. Without thinking, Sam dove onto her. The only thought he had was — get the medallion. With both hands, he wrestled with her, struggling mightily to get the medallion from her grasp.

Aurelia shrieked straight into his ear, using her other hand to rake his back with her claws. The painful sound made everything in Sam's vision explode into a bright white light, but he didn't stop. He squeezed her wrist and bent her fingers with everything he had until, finally, the medallion came free!

Sam jumped off of her and rolled onto his knees.

Aurelia coiled up on her tail and lunged.

"Sam!" Alex was several paces away and threw the hatchet towards Sam. It landed just a couple inches from him.

Aurelia was mere feet from Sam, both claws raised toward the sky, but when Sam flung the medallion to the sand and lifted the hatchet overhead, she stopped screaming.

Fear pierced her eyes. Her hateful glare raced from the medallion to the Viking hatchet to Sam. She closed her eyes. Her trembling stopped.

Again, her face morphed back to the way she had looked when Sam first met her. Her face scrunched in concentration as she held the magical transformation. Her entire body changed back to its original, mermaid beauty. Sam couldn't help it. He felt love in his heart for this girl.

"Please. Sammy," the beautiful mermaid said as she opened her eyes. "My wonderful Sammy."

Alex and Ethan were yelling from down the beach, but Sam couldn't hear them. He could hear nothing except Aurelia's sweet, tinkling voice.

"I was wrong. You were right. I should not have taken this path with your sister. I see that now."

"Uh… I'm glad to hear that," Sam whispered.

Aurelia smiled and Sam's heart bulged with the glory of her magnificent beauty.

"But we can be together, Sam. Together forever. There is still a way."

"How?" Sam gasped, with hopefulness. "I'll help you."

"I know you will. Only you understand me, Sammy. Only you love me."

Sam blinked at her as Aurelia inched closer toward him.

"Tell me how to help," Sam said.

"All you have to do is tell me who."

"Who?" Sam scrunched up his face, not understanding. "Who what?"

"Who you want me to be," Aurelia smiled sweetly.

Then her face transformed again. This time, it was Jessica. Aurelia's body was the same beautiful mermaid body, but now the face was Jessica's.

She was even closer now. Her arms started to raise, palms up, as if begging… reaching…

"Just tell me who you want, Sam. You can have any girl. Just help me."

Sam's body deflated. His hope vanished. Aurelia felt it. Sam looked down at the medallion, pulsing there in front of him in all its hypnotic beauty.

Sam sighed, "If there was some other way. Any other way. I'd do it. Not because of love, but because of pity."

Aurelia's eyes flashed darkly, "Pity?! You *pity* me?"

Sam nodded. "Now I realize who the real you is. I don't love you. I only thought I did."

Aurelia shifted back to her beautiful mermaid face. She inched even closer, raised her arms a little higher.

"Come on, Sam. Look at me. Remember. Remember what you felt when you first met me."

"I do. But what's inside you—it needs help, Aurelia. You may have been the most beautiful girl I've ever seen in my life, but that isn't enough. Deep inside, you are evil!"

A tear ran down the mermaid's fair cheek. "But I'll change and you can have me forever."

Sam sniffled. "I won't help you possess someone. I just can't."

"Okay, Sam." Aurelia's face hardened and she changed back to her true form.

Her lips pulled back, revealing sharp fangs of teeth.

"If you won't help me... then you'll die!"

Springing off of her powerful tail, Aurelia lunged through the air, claws reaching for Sam's neck and her mouthful of teeth open and ready to rip apart his face.

In that moment, Sam lifted his arm and with one swing, he brought the hatchet down onto the medallion. Loud thunder erupted from the medallion as the Viking hatchet connected with it.

A brilliant flash of green energy surged, blinding everyone temporarily.

A hundred bolts of lightning burst out from the medallion.

Sam was thrown backwards from the impact of the powerful explosion.

Then… everything went black.

***

Sam's ears were still ringing from the explosion's impact. As he slowly opened his stinging eyes, everything looked blurry. Sam squinted until things began to focus. Right above him was his sister, Leah. She was clearly out of the trance.

"Hey... Munchkin?"

Leah scooped her arms around her little brother and squeezed him tight. Alex and his parents were staring down at him, concerned, but now elated. Sam pulled himself onto his elbows.

Alex shouted, "You're all right!"

"Wait... where's Ethan?" Sam asked with concern.

Ethan came from behind Sam slowly, cradling something in his arms. A small squeak came from what he was carrying.

Sam looked closer and saw —

"Sagitta!" Sam's heart leapt to his throat to see the majestic bird being carried like a baby. "Is she...okay?"

"She'll live," Mrs. Fisher said. "She has a broken wing. But things heal. Most things."

Sam reached out and pet the bird's head. Sagitta leaned into his fingers, affectionately. Her feathers fluffed up.

"She saved my life," Sam whispered.

And you saved them all, Young Warrior. Sam heard Mr. Brown's voice echo through his mind.

"Where's Aurelia?" Sam asked, not sure he wanted to know the answer.

"She disappeared in the flash," Ethan said.

"No," Alex said. "I'm sure I saw her thrown into the lake."

Sam turned to the Fishers.

Mr. Fisher shrugged. "We thought you might be able to help with that one. The flash of light was so bright, none of us can say for sure."

"I heard a splash," Ethan said confidently. "Her body definitely hit the water."

"And the medallion?" Sam asked, not seeing it anywhere around him. Alex looked down at the ground. Ethan shrugged.

"I... I heard two splashes," Leah said forebodingly, gazing out at the lake.

Sam swallowed. "Does that mean..."

Mr. Fisher stood up tall. "We don't know exactly what that means."

"But hey," Ethan chirped. "We're alive! That's gotta count for something!"

"It indubitably does!" Alex said.

Ethan laughed. "Indubitably!" he repeated as he wrapped his arm around Alex's shoulder.

"But…" Sam took a breath. "But what if she's still out there? And what if the medallion is out there too, damaged but not destroyed?"

All of them turned to look out at the icy waters of Moon Lake. Sagitta gave a piercing cry.

Even though the hawk was cradled in Ethan's arms, it was the bravest, most powerful sound Sam had ever heard. The magnificent bird continued to stare out at the lake as if on the lookout for danger.

"She's right," Sam said, staring at Sagitta.

"Oh, really?" Leah chuckled. "You speak hawk now?"

Sam playfully shrugged off her comment and concluded, "Well, if she's out there, with or without the medallion, we'll be here to face her."

Seven pairs of strong, brave eyes scanned the lake. Sagitta gave one more heart-lifting cry, as if agreeing.

CHAPTER THIRTY

The Voice

Summer at Moon Lake was peaceful. The air was fresh with the fragrance of wild flowers and green vegetation. Everything was brimming with life and the evening sky bloomed with warm, inviting colors.

Sam dangled his bare feet off the dock and dipped his toes into the warm water. He carefully watched the surface of the lake. Since the springtime, there hadn't been a single occurrence of the mermaid's haunting noises. It seemed that everyone had gotten back into the routine of things and forgotten about the strange things that happened at the lake in the early spring. Two dragonflies passed by and landed on one of the reeds. As Sam looked closer at the reeds, he saw something silvery flash underwater.

His heart skipped a beat and goosebumps covered his arms. When he looked closer, he only saw underwater seaweed. Sam took a deep breath and shook his head.

He took a moment to embrace the beauty of the lake. He realized he had been overthinking everything since his last encounter with the mermaid. After all, nothing mysterious had happened at the lake since the final battle.

"Aurelia is defeated," Sam whispered to himself. *We're all safe now.*

Sam heard a voice behind him say, "Hey, Sammy. How are you doing?"

Sam turned around to see Jessica walking down the fishing dock, alone.

"Oh, hi Jessica. How's your summer been?" Sam said nervously. "I haven't seen you since the end of the school year."

Jessica took her shoes off and sat next to Sam. She also dipped her feet into the water and looked out into the horizon. Many people were swimming in the lake. At the nearby playground, kids were flying kites and running. The smell of delicious barbeques filled the air.

"Yes, that's true." Jessica blushed. "I have been meaning to tell you that I'm sorry about everything that happened before… at school… I didn't mean for it to happen like that."

"Oh, uh. That's okay." Sam hesitated, looking down at his knees, and then shrugged. "I mean, like, don't worry about it."

"You know," Jessica continued. "It was all Briana and Stacy's idea." Her eyelashes fluttered effortlessly. "I'm really sorry. I hope we can still be friends."

Sam looked up into Jessica's eyes — and shuttered. For a moment, it was as if Sam saw Aurelia's face in place of Jessica's. He clenched his eyes shut.

Opening them again, Sam stared at Jessica and clearly saw Aurelia's glowing eyes looking straight through him. What used to be Jessica's long brown hair looked like it had a tint of silver to it. Sam jumped to his feet and stood, speechless, with his mouth open.

"Uh... Sam, you alright?" Jessica asked skeptically. She rose to her feet. "You look like you just saw a ghost."

Sam blinked and then looked back at Jessica. He didn't see Aurelia anymore, only Jessica in all of her simple beauty. She looked so lovely in her yellow and white dress. Sam shook his head and exhaled loudly. His eyes had been playing tricks on him.

After all, it was silly for him to believe he had seen Aurelia.

That was impossible.

"Yeah," Sam stammered. "Sorry. It's nothing." Sam shrugged and then straightened his shoulders. "I, uh, thought I saw something."

Jessica blinked at him quizzically. An awkward silence passed between them.

"So, what are you up to today?" Sam asked, trying to keep the conversation casual.

"I've just been enjoying these last days of summer with my family. Speaking of, how is your sister doing?" Jessica gently touched Sam's hand.

"She's..."

Then Jessica whispered, "Too bad I couldn't take her."

"What?!" Sam's voice shook. "What did you say?" He yanked his hand from Jessica's.

"What's gotten into you?" Jessica asked, confused. "I just said I'm sorry about what happened to your sister."

Sam blushed. "I totally misheard you."

"You're funny," Jessica said with a laugh as she got up. "Anyway, I'll catch you around. See you soon, Sammy!"

Jessica winked and then walked away. Sam watched Jessica in awe. As she walked, he heard her laugh again. This time, it echoed through his ears, a familiar laugh. Very familiar. It sounded like—like bubbles rising from the ocean.

There was no mistaking that laugh, that voice.

It was Aurelia's voice. Or was it?

Made in United States
North Haven, CT
02 April 2022

17795650R10171